WITHDRAWN

WARREN'S
OLDE STYLE

Gaudeamus
Igitur

Alois Jirásek

Gaudeamus Igitur

GREENWOOD PRESS, PUBLISHERS
WESTPORT, CONNECTICUT

Library of Congress Cataloging in Publication Data

Jirásek, Alois, 1851-1930.
  Gaudeamus igitur.

  Translation of Filosofská historie.
  Reprint of the 1961 ed. published by Artia, Prague, in
series: Artia pocket books.
    I.   Title.
[PZ3.J568Gau4] [PG5038.J5] 891.8'6'35   76-58010
ISBN 0-8371-9469-5

Gaudeamus Igitur

(Filosofská historie)

by ALOIS JIRÁSEK

translated

by ERIKA VILÍMOVÁ

First Edition

© 1961

by ARTIA PRAGUE

Originally published in 1961 by Artia, Prague

Reprinted with the permission of The Heirs of the
Estate of Alois Jirasek

Reprinted in 1977 by Greenwood Press, Inc.

Library of Congress catalog card number   76-58010

ISBN 0-8371-9469-5

Printed in the United States of America

1

My story opens in 1847 towards the end of April. Spring had come delightfully early that year, with warm days and a cloudless sky. The trees in the Litomyšl Manor park were in full bloom and frail green leaves trembled in the sun. The towers and spires of the Piarist Church, the many roofs and cupolas showed clearly in the bright, transparent air. The roads and streets were gritty, and the rough paving of the large town-square was completely dry. The houses were bathed in sunshine and even the archways running on both sides of the square were warmly lit.

The archways were crowded with young people, who could no more resist the lovely spring afternoon than a bird can resist the sun. Their laughter and their noise did not disturb the town constable, Mr Kmoníček, who was peacefully asleep on a stone bench in the sun. He was past his prime, and quite undeniably preferred resting to any kind of work. It was obvious that he was on his return journey from one of the town's suburbs where he had been with an announcement. The drum was slung across his shoulder, and the drumsticks inside their yellow holsters were pushed well inside the leather strap. He was well-known for his weakness of sleeping whenever and wherever

7

he had the chance, immaterial whether standing up or sitting down, and it was even said that he slept while walking. His hat was pushed down well over his forehead, his chin sunk onto his chest, and the sounds of honest, healthy snoring came forth from under his close-clipped moustache.

These sounds did not disturb Miss Elis who was sitting at an open window on the first floor, right above Kmoníček. Miss Elis was — to use plain language — a spinster, whose kind, faded blue eyes had watched the return of spring fifty times or more.

She sat at the window, knitting a stocking and noticing neither the bright blue sky nor the lovely sunshine. She did not even glance at the people moving across the square, and yet her needles did not click as busily or as regularly as usual. Her hands would often drop onto her lap, while her eyes wandered around the room, now watching the door which led to the other room, then again looking at the clock with its alabaster pillars, placed on the chest of drawers, whose yellow brass ornaments shone like gold.

Everything in Miss Elis's room gleamed, not a speck of dust was to be seen, nor even a shadow of disorder, things stood in their place neatly and tidily. The chairs and sofas with their freshly clean upholstery were of old-fashioned, eighteenth century style; but the round table, covered with a brightly coloured table-cloth, and the other furniture the room contained were more up-to-date already, fashionable during the last years of the Republic and Napoleon's reign.

The time was nearly five o'clock. Miss Elis placed her knitting and the wool on the window ledge and walked towards the door, where she stopped, hesitating. An indistinguishable murmur came from the other side, and she stood there for a few moments debating whether to knock.

Suddenly the talk came to an abrupt end, and a young man of average height stood in the doorway.

'Mr Vavřena, it's long past four o'clock, whatever are you up to? What will your pupil's parents think of you?'

'You're quite right, Miss Elis.' The youth, whose name was Frybort, added smilingly, 'I'm having trouble with him; he's fallen in love with his ideas and I can't make him stop discussing them.'

'What ideas?'

'Oh, mostly secret plans and revolutions and suchlike. He'd like to blow up the whole of Litomyšl.'

'Good gracious, Mr Frybort, the things you say!'

'I'm just about to go, Miss Elis,' said Vavřena, who appeared behind Frybort in the doorway. He was a student of philosophy, a tall, slim youth with an expressive face. He was ready to leave, hat in hand.

'I really can't think what's come over you, Mr Vavřena, that you could so forget the time. You're so punctual as a rule.'

Vavřena smiled. 'Oh, I'll make up for it, you'll see.'

'Hurry up, do; Miss Lottie looks very charming today, I saw her at the window. She looked very pretty in her light dress and with pink ribbons in her hair.'

'My dear Frybort, I'm sure I don't know what Márinka would say if she were to hear you discussing light dresses and pink ribbons.'

'Oh, but Miss Elis won't tell on me, will you?' drawled Frybort, smiling cheerfully.

Vavřena left. Miss Elis, whose lodgers Vavřena and Frybort were, sat down again and picked up her knitting. Frybort had not moved from the door to his room.

'Hasn't Zelenka been home yet this afternoon?'

9

'No, he hasn't,' Miss Elis replied. 'Poor lad, he spends all his time giving lessons. I think he's having rather a hard time. He asked me to make a fruit stew and I have a whole plateful of dried fruit in the kitchen waiting for him; I don't know how he manages to keep his strength up.'

'True enough, and he works much harder than is really necessary, too.'

Miss Elis, looking up from her knitting, smiled at the student. 'Studying certainly seems to agree with you more than it does with him. There's something else I've been meaning to ask you, though, Mr Frybort; have you noticed anything out of the ordinary about Mr Špína?'

'No, I don't think so, why?'

'Well, it's rather surprising that you haven't noticed anything, because to me he seems so lost in thought, and he's been awfully quiet lately.'

'Oh, I shouldn't worry about that, if I were you. That's probably because he's to enter a monastery so soon.'

'Oh no, I'm sure it isn't that, although I know he doesn't want to enter it. I believe it's something that goes much deeper than this. Shall I tell you what I think? I believe he's fallen in love!'

'Špína — in love?' Frybort said incredulously and burst into such honest laughter that even Miss Elis had to smile.

'How I'd like to watch him bend down from his great height to kiss his sweetheart!'

'Oh, how mean of you!'

'No, I'm not being mean, I think Špína is a good fellow. It's only that I can't imagine it. If I were sure that you were right I just couldn't help laughing.'

'Mr Frybort, you won't say anyting to him, will you?'

'Where is he, by the way?'

'He took his book and said he'd study. He complained he was too busy.'

10

'Of course he's busy — if he's in love.'

'And what about you, Mr Frybort, I've never heard *you* complain yet!'

'Why should *I* complain! To me, love is a sweet burden which I can never have enough of — and as for my studies, why, there's all the time in the world till the end of the year. But Miss Elis —' His easy flow of words ceased as he looked at the chest of drawers, above which a small, round oil painting had been placed.

It was a portrait of a young priest, against a blurred, dark background. It was not the picture itself that had caught his attention, for he was used to seeing it in its place every day. A small half-wreath of moss and artificial flowers had been put above the picture and seemed to be touching the young priest's head.

'Surely that wreath didn't use to be there,' Frybort said as he looked questioningly at Miss Elis. She sat in her chair, motionless, her hands folded in her lap. Her gaze faltered and a slight flush crept across her faded cheeks when Frybort looked at the picture with such obvious surprise.

'You see, it's St George's day today, and his name was George —'

The teasing smile vanished from the student's face. Just then they both heard quick steps on the staircase, the door opened and a thin, pale youth entered the room. His 'good afternoon' was said in passing as he hurried next door to the room which he shared with Vavřena, Frybort and Špína.

'I say, what's the hurry, old boy,' Frybort asked.

'It's almost five o'clock, that's the time for my next lesson and I forgot my books.' With that he disappeared through the door.

'Who'd be a tutor!' Frybort sighed and, as if moved

11

by Zelenka's example, he said to Miss Elis, 'I have work to do, too,' and followed Zelenka, who had already found the books and hurried from the house to teach his young charge the necessary school pensum.

Frybort sat down at his table which was littered with an untidy heap of books and papers, dipped his quill into the ink and began to write on a clean sheet of paper.

'Fellow-students!' Big, black letters showed up against the white paper.

A deep silence settled upon the rooms. Miss Elis lifted her head, frowning slightly, and went on with her knitting.

The silence was shattered suddenly, as some unknown little rascal beat old Kmoníček's drum. The constable, having thus been torn from his slumbers, rose rather sleepily and continued his interrupted journey to the town-hall.

Meanwhile, Vavřena hurried towards his pupil's home. He passed archways and Jew's Hill, the Manor, the grammar-school and the Piarist college; finally, he entered a dark house built in eighteenth-century style. Stag's horns adorned the wall above the entrance to this patrician house, and a 'God's eye' with long, yellowish rays had been painted underneath.

The staircase was dark and, when Vavřena arrived on the first floor, he stopped and knocked on one of the doors. No sound came from within, no one answered. He entered.

A young lady, seated at the table, was taken completely by surprise. As soon as she heard the door open she rose from her chair hurriedly, and hid something under the dress material which lay spread out on the table. It was obvious that she had not been attending to her sewing.

She blushed deeply and did not turn her head until she recognized Vavřena's voice. Then she said in a pleasant, friendly voice:

'Oh, it's you, Mr Vavřena. You gave me such a shock,' she added candidly.

'I'm so sorry. Is Fricek not at home?'

'Oh dear, you startled me so much I nearly forgot to give you the message. He went out with Auntie and with Lottie, and Auntie told me to ask you to wait for them. They won't be long, I think.'

'Of course.' The reply came promptly, and the student's expression as well as his voice showed that he would be pleased to wait. Pointing to the room where Fricek had his lessons as a rule, she said:

'Would you care to go in there?'

'Would I be very much in the way if I stayed here with you?'

The girl blushed again, but smiled and pointed to a chair, which Vavřena took readily.

Lenka had really been taken by surprise, and she still felt rather flustered and confused, which became her immensely. She snatched up her work again as if to make up for lost time, but this was only a pretence to cover her embarrassment. While looking for her needle or her scissors — goodness only knows how it came about — she touched the material lightly, and part of it slid off the table. There was a thud as something hard fell on the floor.

Lenka bent down quickly, trying to retrieve it, but Vavřena, who had also stooped, picked it up before she had a chance to touch it.

Their hands met and Vavřena felt the touch of the smooth, velvety skin of her cheek against his temple.

Dark colour flooded her face again.

The book fell open. 'May I have a look at the title?'

13

Gazing at the student with her beautiful clear eyes, Lenka kept silent. He held the slim volume in his hands and read aloud:

ALMANAC
or
NEW YEAR'S CALENDAR FOR 1823

Unconsciously he released the pages he had been holding between his thumb and forefinger, and looked at the lines of prose and verse, till finally his eyes came to rest on Lenka's face again.

'I beg your pardon for doing you a great wrong, even in my mind. I saw you hide something, and to tell the truth I thought it was a letter —'

'A letter? I'd like to know who from,' and Lenka smiled, showing her white, even teeth.

'It wouldn't be so surprising, would it,' the student laughed, matching her gay mood. 'Do you know, though, a Czech book was the last thing I expected to see. You don't know how surprised I am. I think if I asked every girl I know I wouldn't find one who owns a book written in her mother tongue. I'd no idea you were a patriot. You are, aren't you?' he asked, holding out his hand to her.

'Yes, I am,' came the firm reply, and Vavřena pressed the small soft hand which trembled lightly.

'May I ask who lent you the New Year's Calendar?'

'Oh, I own quite a number of them. Have you read this one yet?'

'You put me to shame — but I must admit I haven't.'

'Then take it, if you like. I've read it twice already, and have been leafing through it now. I've got several more in my bag and you can have them all if you like. But you'll have to pay me back in kind, I warn you.'

14

'I'll be delighted to lend you anything I have, but I'm afraid it doesn't amount to much.'

'You will be careful, won't you, that neither Auntie nor Lottie find out about it. Perhaps you understand now why I hid the book so quickly when I heard someone at the door. Auntie doesn't care for me to read at all and ridicules Czech books particularly. Don't think I'm a coward, I do have the courage of my convictions, but since I mustn't answer Auntie back I try not to give any cause for talk.'

'Try and bear it, Lenka, it's a good cause you're fighting for. You can't imagine how happy I am to have really got to know you today. Believe me, I writhe with shame when I watch our young ladies and when I listen to them. Their frivolous talk of ribbons and laces, their tattling in a foreign tongue, their meaningless phrases learned from foreign books, all these things drive me to distraction. They don't think it fashionable and elegant enough to talk and read in their mother tongue, or to betray any patriotic feeling. And to think that these are the mothers of our future generation! Small wonder the children are growing up indifferent to the nation's fate. These young ladies are supposed to have a kind and soft heart and yet, it's made of stone where the century-old misery of their own nation is concerned.'

Lenka sat quite still, hardly daring to breathe, and looked at him with shining eyes. His words, uttered with such conviction, went straight to her heart. She took a deep breath, and a happy smile spread over her features, while her eyes filled with tears.

'Thank you, oh thank you,' she said quietly after a pause. 'I feel refreshed and braced. Much time has passed since I last heard words like yours. My late uncle used to talk to me like that too.

'Your late uncle! Was he your teacher?'

'These books used to be his, he left them to me.'

'Would you like to tell me about him?'

'Yes, I would, but —' Voices sounded in the hall and Lenka, startled, picked up her sewing hurriedly. 'Auntie —'

Whereupon the door opened and the mistress of the house entered, accompanied by her daughter and young Fricek.

'*Ach schau, Lottie,* Mr Vavřena is still waiting for us. I'm sorry we've kept you waiting, *aber es ist so schön draussen.*' Vavřena, who was bowing politely, had no chance to interrupt her lively flow of words.

The ladies stayed in the room, while tutor and pupil left to go next door, where papers and books lay waiting for them.

Mrs Roubínek was a tall, handsome woman, whose face did not give away her years. Her black, well-groomed hair was as smooth as her daughter's, and Lottie was the image of her mother. She was rightly considered one of the prettiest young ladies of the town. Dark eyes set in a lovely face, together with a slim figure did much to make her more attractive than the other girls. Apart from that she dressed tastefully and well, and Mamma spared no expense. Mr Roubínek gave in willy-nilly, although he was rather stingy otherwise.

Lenka had time enough to calm down and to show a serene face, while mother and daughter took off their shawls and bonnets. She sewed diligently, answering her aunt's questions in her usual quiet manner. Her mind, however, was far from calm. Long ago her young heart had started to beat faster at the thought of the student who was so popular among his friends and colleagues. She felt pleased whenever she caught a glimpse of him when he came to teach Fricek, and was happy when he addressed a few words to her on those occasions. She had thought

16

that it was the pure Czech he spoke which had attracted her so much, and which only one other person in all her acquaintance had used. That person had been her uncle. Her aunt and Lottie too were full of praise for Vavřena and it gave her pleasure to listen to their talk; she herself, however, dared not mention him to anyone.

She had received a very pleasant surprise that afternoon. It had never occurred to her before that he might have any understanding for her beliefs and ideals, much less share them or even praise her for them. She was used to hiding her innermost thoughts, for of late they had been a source of amusement to others. But he had held her hand and said: 'You can't imagine how happy I am to have really got to know you today!'

Apart from being a true and ardent patriot she was also very much a woman. On previous occasions it had given her pleasure to look at the handsome student who was so well thought of by Lottie and her friends. But today he, who was so indifferent to girls otherwise, had stood in front of her, sincere, his face lit as if by an inner glow. If Lottie or her friends could have seen him then and listened to his enraptured speech, they would hardly have stayed indifferent and their hearts would have softened, even if they did not share his ideals.

The impression was all the greater on Lenka, the Cinderella of the house whom no one took much notice of and appreciated even less. Her parents had died in her early youth, and the orphaned child had been cared for by her uncle, the parish priest of a forgotten little village high up in the hills. He had been her mother's eldest brother, and one of the few patriotic men who, in those times of stress and almost complete apathy, did his good work quietly, though to the benefit of the whole community

Lenka had been his ward; on his death she inherited —

apart from his whole library — only a small sum of money. Mr Roubínek, who was another brother of her mother's, took her into his family. A year had passed since she had entered the household of her second uncle, where she had become a companion to Miss Lottie, who was the apple of her mother's eye.

When the appointed time for the lesson had passed Vavřena returned to the front room, ready to take his leave. Mrs Roubínek, however, kept him. She enjoyed talking to him and immediately started a conversation in her usual hotchpotch of languages, beginning a sentence in Czech and adding German words to it as if trying to make her meaning clearer. She asked the tutor if he too had made the best of this beautiful day, and told him where she and Lottie had been for a walk and how enchanting the park looked. And of course, she had to mention how enthralled Lottie had been. '*Sie war hin vor Bewunderung!*' she added.

Lottie said: 'And this is only April! Can you imagine what May will be like?'

Vavřena moved slightly.

'I cannot think what's come over the authorities! What pleasure the first of May used to give people! *Diese Majales!*'

'Won't there be any again this year, Mr Vavřena?' Lottie asked.

Her mother replied instead of him: 'How could there be? They were forbidden last year, and I'm sure they won't be allowed this year either.'

'Oh, but maybe they will,' the student said unexpectedly firmly. Lottie said 'oh' and sighed contentedly, giving him a searching look.

'And so they should be, too. They're as old as philosophy itself, *es ist ihr Vorrecht!*'

'What a lot of fun they used to be!' Lottie repeated, looking dreamily at nothing in particular as if she were seeing thrilling pictures of the delightful students' festival. 'Dear Mr Vavřena, you will do your best, won't you, to see that the *Majales* are celebrated again this year!'

'I'm giving it a lot of thought, madam,' Vavřena smiled.

He took his leave at last and glanced fleetingly at Lenka, whose head was bent low over her sewing. She felt his glance and her heart leaped.

Lottie said cheerfully: 'I've just remembered, Mamma, that Mina told me something about Mr Vavřena this morning.'

'Well, my love? And what did she have to say?'

'She said that Mr Vavřena might be ever so nice and even handsome, and that if he weren't *so stolz, so könnte man ihn ausstehen.*'

'Nothing but envy and *Eifersucht*, I assure you.' And she looked at her daughter significantly.

19

2

Frybort was engrossed in his work. He wrote, crossed out, corrected what he had just put down, thought things over and wrote again. He was so absorbed by his task that he was quite deaf to all the noise from the town square and the archways below.

The room was a typical students' room, not large, bare of ornaments, but furnished comfortably. Most of the space was taken up by four bedsteads and a black trunk standing beside each one of them. There were two large tables and a smaller one, the latter serving Frybort for his writing, and a bookcase against the further wall. Two framed coloured copper engravings, copies of French Masters hung on the wall, and a guitar adorned with a green ribbon had been placed between them.

Frybort had almost finished reading the draft in its final form, when he heard Miss Elis's mild voice in the hall, and another, deeper one, answering her. He folded the paper hurriedly and pushed it far back into the table-drawer; no sooner had he done this, when a tall young man with a slight stoop entered. He had been born with limbs as straight as any other child's, and his stoop was the result of endless sitting about and the way he walked.

'Well, well, so you are home at last. Where on earth do you keep disappearing to?'

'Nowhere, I was in the park,' answered Špína, for that was his name. He sat down on the trunk and, picking up a piece of bread from the large table, he attacked it with great zeal.

Frybort watched his friend in silence. Špína picked up his book after a few bites and was engrossed in it in no time. His face was very unattractive: a mud-coloured complexion and a low forehead, an ugly nose coupled with buck teeth made him anything but handsome.

A few minutes passed in silence. 'I say, Špína,' Frybort started.

'Can't you see I'm studying? Leave me alone,' his friend answered curtly. Barely five minutes later, however, he threw the book across the room and jumped to his feet.

'To hell with all philosophy!'

'My, my, what a temper! Why the excitement?'

'Temper indeed! I'm sure you wouldn't be calm either if you were in my place. I almost work my fingers to the bone with the only result that I get a good mark now and then, but what's the difference? It's the monastery for me whatever happens, don't you see? But I won't be a monk I tell you, I won't, I won't!' he stormed.

'For heaven's sake! What's come over you? Come here for a minute, will you?'

'Oh, leave me alone.'

'I won't leave you alone. As a matter of fact I won't let you get away now until you answer me. Come on, make a clean breast of it and tell me: you're in love, aren't you?'

Špína's simple swarthy face turned scarlet with embarrassment. 'What do you mean? How ... where —'

'Oh, come on. Won't you take me into your confidence?'

21

'Take you into my confidence! The very idea!'

Špína was an easy-going fellow as a rule and not in the habit of answering so sulkily. Now he turned away and sat down again. Frybort saw how irritated he was and said no more. After a while, he picked up his hat and asked:

'I suppose you don't know whether Márinka is in the shop or whether her mother is there, do you?'

'No, I don't,' Špína mumbled and the colour rushed to his face again.

Frybort passed through Miss Elis's room, which was empty as Miss Elis was in the kitchen. He stood above the narrow, winding staircase from which the afternoon light had already faded.

Suddenly a gay song floated up from the ground-floor, followed by quick, light footsteps on the stairs. Frybort took a few steps down and opened his arms wide, touching the wall with his fingertips on both sides of the staircase. The girl who was coming up in a hurry bumped into him, and a faint cry sounded in the dusk.

'Márinka, it's only me.'

'Oh, do let me pass, please. Mummy is downstairs in the shop and —'

'And we're here where she can neither see nor hear us.'

'Look, I've got a bunch of violets here which I meant to put into water. I'll let you have them if you'll let me pass. I'll buy myself off with them, since you're so mean.'

'All right, that'll suit me nicely.'

'Well, here you are, take them. But —' Silence followed as he embraced her.

'That's for the flowers,' he said, his lips brushing her temple and her smooth, rosy cheeks. She stayed still in his arms only for a short moment; suddenly she drew away and, with a few steps, stood above him on the stairs. Her

22

eyes were bright and her cheeks were flushed, her hair was disarranged.

'Márinka, will you come for a walk with me?' the eager youth asked in a low voice.

'I'm cross with you.'

'Will you come to the park or would you prefer to go to the palisades?'

'I'd rather go to the park —' and with that she disappeared into the room next to Miss Elis's. Frybort's pulses quickened as he held the flowers in his hand. He left the house. There was a grocer's to the right, where Márinka stood behind the counter every afternoon. Now her mother was there. She had given Márinka permission to spend the afternoon with a friend. Frybort's 'good afternoon' was very polite as he passed her.

'Why, Mr Frybort!'

He stopped.

'What have you been doing, you're all white!' the worthy matron said as she pointed to his chest, where a fine white dust had settled on his coat.

'Dear me, that's nothing. I seem to have brushed against a wall, that's all.'

'Oh? And did you brush against it with your chest?'

'I expect I didn't put the coat away any too tidily.' And laughingly he took his leave of the good lady, who looked at him askance.

'I forgot that Márinka was a flower among flour at the shop. Now I think of it, even her hair looks as if it were powdered,' he thought happily as he turned his steps towards the Manor park.

Evening fell. The students' room was lit by a table-lamp and a candle stood on the smaller table, by the light of which Vavřena sat reading. Špína, fully dressed, lay on his

23

back, stretched across the untidy bed in a gloomy corner, and pulled at his pipe.

He lay there staring at the wall with unseeing eyes.

Silence hung over the room; it was disturbed by nothing but the occasional tinkling of a spoon. Zelenka was having his evening meal, fruit stew and a slice of bread. It was his third slice already, but the last one for the day. He had rationed his bread for the morning, noon and evening meal, and adhered strictly to this self-imposed rule. His food consisted of little else but bread. He had just left his last pupil of the day, and felt tired and hungry, and quite enjoyed the scanty meal. He had hardly finished eating and clearing the table when he began to study again, or — as Frybort was fond of putting it — he swotted.

Vavřena was very interested in Lenka's *Almanac*. He held it in his hand without reading it, while he looked thoughtfully at the cover, which bore a Gothic inscription on paper turning yellow with age:

„Und weh dem Lande, dessen Söhne
frech verachten Heimatstöne
und heimatlichen Sagenkreis!"

A little lower down, there was another inscription in ordinary writing:

'*My country! Thy doom is grief unsurpassed.*'
Myslimír.

These words gave food for thought. They had been written by Lenka's uncle, the priest, whose patriotic pseudonym was Myslimír.

How he must have suffered before he had written down these words which seemed so bereft of hope. His love for his country, ever-alive even in the forgotten little village high up in the mountains, his faith in the future, his fears and his distress, and his final, bleak dispair. Could

24

the words have expressed only a momentary depression, had he really believed up to the last moments of his life that the nation was doomed, or did these words contain the sad truth?

Vavřena could not, would not believe it. No, never! Times had been worse and clouds had looked even blacker, and yet, the nation had survived. The heavy fog, so all-enfolding, was slowly lifting, pierced here and there by rays of sunshine. The sun would break through in the end and then — oh then, what glorious, bright days lay ahead!

Again, and yet again his eyes turned to those desperate words. In his mind's eye he saw the grave, aging priest sitting in the rectory garden, well shaded by bushy trees. A girl sat beside him and — yes, he saw it clearly — she was reading to the priest, while he listened, explaining something now and then, till finally she fell silent and he told her tales of the nation's glorious past. And she sat entranced, listening, with eyes as shining as they had been today, while she had listened to him breathlessly, full of wonder. The book fell open, the writing on the cover disappeared.

'PINDAR AND CORINNA'

Awaking from his day-dreams, Vavřena began to read the first story.

'The Morning Star is luminous in the East and the Evening Star shines brightly in the West. Once upon a time both stars twinkled in the skies of Greece.

'Corinna was begotten by Tanagra, Pindar by Thebes.'

He read no further than the introduction to this tender tale of love, for he was disturbed by Frybort who entered the quiet room noisily, humming a tune under his breath.

'I say, Vavřena, have you read it yet?'

'Yes, I have, and I've made a few corrections. I've shortened it a little, too.'

'That's all right. Here, what do you think of this? Isn't it a nice little bunch of flowers?'

'Yes, it is, why?'

'It's a gift, and I should say a gift of the Gods. Would you like to smell them?'

'No, I wouldn't, I want to read.'

'Well then, you have a look, Zelenka.'

'Why don't you let me get on with my studies?'

'All right, all right. You smell them, Špína, and see how quickly you'll be cured of your bad temper. They're really lovely and, what's more, Márinka gave them to me.'

Špína, who had been about to get up, sank back onto the bed and turned his head away, mumbling.

'Oh, you bookworms! Aren't you a dull lot!' Frybort exclaimed, as he put the flowers in water. Having done this, he jumped on the trunk and took the guitar off the wall.

Zelenka put his hands over his ears and bent lower over his book as soon as he saw that the guitar was being tuned. Frybort strummed a few chords and, having settled down comfortably on his bed, started to sing in his deep, melodious voice:

'Darkness had fallen
when I saw Márinka home —'

Zelenka looked at his noisy friend beseechingly, and in desperation started to recite his part in an undertone. Frybort, however, was quite undeterred. The guitar was slung across his shoulder and he plucked at the strings and sang about Márinka, whom he had taken home.

26

3

On Sunday morning Vavře-
na and Frybort were seated at the small table, where they
re-read and discussed the paper which Frybort had written
and which Vavřena had corrected. It was very early in the
morning and Špína was fast asleep still, whereas Zelenka
was already engrossed in his studies. They talked quietly,
almost in whispers, no third person could have caught
a word. Apart from that Zelenka was really so taken up
by his studies that he took no notice whatsoever of his
whispering friends.

'We'll have to do it that way, otherwise we'll be the
laughing-stock of the place,' Frybort argued.

'The physics students are with us all the way.'

Light, golden in its early-morning freshness, streamed
into the room, forecasting a lovely day. And, as if in praise,
the bells of Dean Church began to chime; their deep,
resonant voices carried well through the bright, clear air.
A little later the grammar-school bell joined with its
penetrating sound. No sooner had it stopped than Vavřena,
fully dressed and cap and cane in hand — for he belonged to
the privileged caste, the students of philosophy — left the
house hurriedly.

'Has anything happened?' Miss Elis asked the rest of

27

her 'family' when they assembled for breakfast. 'Mr Vavřena left without his breakfast, he seemed to be in such a hurry.'

'Perhaps he went for a walk, after all it's a lovely morning,' Frybort replied.

A little later the other students left too.

The time was nine o'clock or thereabouts, and the big hall of the college was filled with students of philosophy — higher grade as well as lower grade — who had come to listen to the sermon.

There were more than three hundred of them. The huge hall was buzzing with young voices, conversation, which was even livelier than usual, went on in German and in Czech and centred around the same subject almost everywhere; there was something in the wind and no one knew where it had started. That, however, was natural enough since April was drawing to its close and the first day of May was about to dawn — the first of May, which had always been so gay and carefree. Since time immemorial, students of philosophy had celebrated their *Majales*, and not only they, but the whole town, old and young alike, looked forward to the traditional students' May Day festival. Two years before the Bishop of Hradec had issued an order forbidding the celebration of the *Majales*. This should have been the third year running without the gaiety and music and without any kind of celebration. May Day was the subject discussed by all and sundry.

Frybort stood at the window opposite the door, where the largest and liveliest group had formed. The door opened and Vavřena entered. As soon as he noticed his friend he made his way towards him; he wanted to avoid the biggest crush and tried to edge past the lecturer's desk. There, however, he stopped as if on a sudden impulse and picked up a sheet of paper which had been placed there, and began to read it quietly.

'Look, fellows, Vavřena has found something.'

'Let's see what you've got there,' someone called.

'It's meant for you in any case.'

The crowd surged forward to the desk. 'We want to see what you've found,' they shouted.

'Read it to us,' other voices joined.

'Silence!' Frybort's voice rose above the din. 'Give Vavřena a chance to read it.'

The noise subsided; Vavřena stood behind the desk and started to read in clear, ringing tones. The paper, whose author was unknown, contained a proclamation addressed to all students of philosophy. It reminded them of the time-honoured tradition and privileges of the students' May Day festival, describing its beauties in glowing words and appealing to their honour and to their reputation as students. It adjured them to be unanimous in their demands and not to succumb to threats, to celebrate their festival with as much splendour as in former days, to resurrect the old privileges and to redeem the honour of the venerable school.

The students shouted whole-hearted approval and agreement and the vast hall filled with a terrific noise. No sooner had Vavřena left the desk to join his friends, when the door opened and the religious instructor walked in. He was a tall thin Piarist, whose cold face wore a habitual frown; his sharp beady eyes noted the extraordinary commotion straight away.

He sat down, and fumbling with his notes, took out a sheet of paper which he unfolded. He announced in his rather squeaky, monotonous voice that, before listening to the sermon, the gentlemen should be made acquainted with an epistle from the Bishop's office. Suppressed humming, sounding like the foreboding of a thunderstorm, came from the back of the hall. The priest went on with the epistle, the gist of which was that the noisy May Day festival was banned again and that this was to remind them of the Bishop's ban which had been issued earlier on.

The storm broke before the priest was half-way through. His voice was drowned in the general uproar, in the booing, hissing, whistling and stamping, banging of canes and furious shouts. A drowning man in a raging thunderstorm had as much chance of making himself heard.

He stopped reading and waited for the noise to subside. But as soon as he picked up the paper again and opened his mouth to resume his reading, pandemonium broke loose. He got to his feet with blazing eyes and tried to address the rows and rows of excited students; when he could not make himself heard even then, he snatched up his papers and left the hall, livid with rage at such humiliation.

The tumult and hubbub went on unabated with shouts of 'Majales! Majales!' rising above the clamour.

The students' Mass which was at nine o'clock was well attended as a rule. Even more people than usual were at church well before nine o'clock on this lovely morning. Gaily coloured dresses rustled in the pews, for the ladies — young and old — attended students' Mass most diligently.

It was well past the time when the service should have started and there was no sign of the students yet. The sexton came out of the sacristy several times and stood in front of the altar, from where he could watch both the main entrance and the side door. Nothing happened.

The candles at the main altar had been burning for some time when there was a hum of voices which heralded

30

the arrival of the students. They streamed into church through the main entrance and the side door.

Many a young lady lifted her head to glance at them, or perhaps to search for one particular face. At any other time she would have lowered her eyes immediately to her prayer-book again; today, however, all eyes were fixed in astonishment on the swarming crowd. Where was their discipline and order? What could have happened? They arrived in disorderly little groups, completely out of line, and to make matters worse, they sat down or stood about just anywhere, in the same undisciplined manner. The congregation's eyes were turned on them in wonder and surprise, for they whispered and murmured and nudged each other with their elbows. The dignified silence which enveloped the church at other times was gone for good that morning.

The bewilderment, however, became greater still when a priest — a member of the college brotherhood — started to celebrate the Mass instead of the religious instructor of the college, who was their own minister.

The students did not disperse after Mass as was their habit; some of them loitered about, others walked away in uncommonly large groups, deep in discussion, gesticulating. The largest group, however, had formed around Frybort and Vavřena.

Mrs Roubínek and her daughter, home from church, discussed the morning's events with animation. Mr Roubínek, getting ready to attend High Mass, which he never missed, listened to their chatter without showing the slightest sign of interest or emotion. He was used to keeping his pale, unimpressive face as expressionless as became a person in his position and as he deemed necessary to uphold his dignity. No one had ever seen any sign of emotion on his impassive, waxen features.

He stood in front of the mirror while mother and daughter chattered away, fingering his white, starched kerchief which he wore tied into a bow; now and again his hands strayed to his hair putting his ringlets into place over his temples. Lottie was in the middle of telling him how disorderly a crowd the students had appeared, when he turned his head and said drily:

'Lenka, I want Aaron please.'

Lenka was greatly impressed by the tale to which she had been listening with interest. Now she got up and went to fetch a dark-blue frock-coat which she handed to her uncle. He put it on with as serious a mien as if he were performing an official act. Mr Roubínek was, above all, a thrifty and a tidy man. And as the squire names his horses, so Mr Roubínek named his coats and frock-coats, which he never wore instinctively or impulsively, but in strict order of succession.

It was Aaron's turn today. The coat had been named after the Jew who had sold him the material — Aaron. There was also an Abraham apart from Aaron, a ginger-coloured coat, bought from the Jew Abraham. However, his wardrobe contained many other coats, which had been given names of Christians.

Whenever there was a feast of the Blessed Virgin, he dressed in blue-grey pantaloons known as 'Mary's' far and wide. There was a time and place for everything in his life, which moved smoothly as if on well-oiled wheels.

Once dressed in Aaron, he picked up his smooth castor and was ready to leave. First he kissed his wife, though coldly, with a deadly serious expression on his face, whereupon he vanished, rigidly stiff in his importance, without another word.

The ladies' tongues began to wag as if they had waited for that moment.

'And to think, Mamma, that Mr Vavřena didn't even bother to turn round to see if we were there!'

'My love, he was no different from the rest. But perhaps he'll put in an appearance in the afternoon, then we'll make him tell us everything, don't worry. *Aber alles!*'

The churchbells were silent, noon had passed.

The family had had their lunch by half past twelve as usual. Fricek ran out into the garden; Lenka, having first helped the maid to clear the table, sat down in the front room to enjoy the quiet Sunday afternoon. This gave her great pleasure. She could do as she liked, while her uncle, Auntie and Lottie were in the back room. She would pick up at random one of the books she had inherited from her uncle and sit by the window and read and read. Occasionally her thoughts would stray to times gone by and a feeling of happiness and freedom would steal over her.

While Lenka sat and read and dreamed, her uncle was comfortably seated in an easy-chair. Aaron had gone to join the other coats, Lottie had filled and lit his long-stemmed pipe for him, smoke curled lazily upwards to the ceiling. Mr Roubínek never smoked except on Sundays, and then only after lunch and towards sundown. He emptied his pipe gravely when all the tobacco had turned into misty smoke and sat down to write his letters. He never did so on any other day; but on Sunday afternoon, when Lottie had gone out to visit friends and Mrs Roubínek was having forty winks, he 'composed' his epistles. Every sentence was well turned over in his mind before being committed to paper with the result that no corrections were ever necessary and his sentences stood like soldiers on parade. On occasion it even took him weeks to complete one letter; he was in no hurry, though, as he did not have a vast amount of correspondence. He would wake his wife as soon as he had finished writing and read to her what he had put on paper. His epistles were dignified and stolid and as dull as ditchwater into the bargain.

Sundays were ever alike, week in, week out.

A little later in the afternoon his friend, the notary, came to visit him, either alone or accompanied by his wife, and the 'entertainment' would begin.

I must inform the reader now of one of Mr Roubínek's peculiarities. Opposite his easy-chair there hung an old picture on the wall in a carved wooden frame. Mr Roubínek considered the picture to be among the most priceless ones in the town, and was even heard to say in a sudden, rare burst of passion: 'There isn't another one like it! It's unrivalled in the whole kingdom!'

Small wonder! The picture portrayed Herod, the cruel, ruthless king, the murderer of Bethlehem's innocent babes and infants. The portrait showed nothing but his head, but it was so well done that the whole brutal deed stared one in the face. Standing under the picture, one saw that the head consisted of nothing but naked infants' bodies; white bodies were used for face and forehead, while black ones made up the hair and beard. Bethlehem must have been full of negroes at the time.

Mr Roubínek was more than proud of this masterpiece, which to him was worth its weight in gold.

While sitting and smoking in his easy-chair, his eyes were fixed upon the picture and stayed there even while he was talking to his wife. What was more, his eyes were glued to King Herod even when visitors were present. It is difficult to say whether it had become a habit or whether his soul was starved for works of art.

Mr Roubínek was very well-to-do for a man of his position. He had married for love — apart from sound reasoning about his bride's aptitude for housekeeping. It

34

would, however, be quite wrong to think that he had been in any way passionate or even affectionate in his youth. In fact, he had not changed at all since then. His friends maintained that not even his looks had changed. Be that as it may, one thing was certain: his wealth came from his uncle's side (he was a military gentleman) and had been amassed during the Napoleonic wars.

This particular Sunday afternoon Mrs Roubínek felt too restless to take her customary nap; her husband pored over his letter, which was addressed to the notary of the Rychmburk estate, who was a friend of his. He wrote his letter in German, not because he held his mother tongue in contempt, but because the words flowed easier from his pen, apart from which his mind was also nimbler in that language. He was no patriot, nor was he their opponent, in fact he was neither friend nor foe. He was a civil servant, heart and soul devoted to his superiors, defending the old order, hating all that was new. Nevertheless, it was obvious from occasional remarks of his that his opinion on historical events differed somewhat from ideas generally held. He did not, for instance, consider Žižka a blackguard and a murderer, as he was mostly thought of then. One of his favourite sayings was: 'Žižka and the Emperor Joseph were the best two Czechs that ever lived.' And when his friend, the notary, nodded in agreement, he continued: 'Our church is a memorial of them.' Since he never mentioned any other historical facts, it seemed that this was the beginning and the end of all he knew of history.

Žižka, the Emperor and, above all, King Herod were the subjects he loved best, although he had never been known to discuss them in any other way than has been mentioned.

Today he had begun his letter and even finished the

35

first paragraph when Lottie ran into the room and came to an abrupt halt at her mother's side. Breathlessly she plunged into her tale, describing to her mother all she had learned from her friend. The town was full of stories similar to the one she told.

The news of the morning's rioting at college had leaked out and even details as to how the sermon had been stopped and the religious instructor had been forced to leave the hall were generally known.

The ladies, both young and old, as well as most of the town's inhabitants were glad to take the students' part. However, those above them in rank and station had begun to shake their heads doubtfully, thinking such actions inexcusable and unpardonable.

'Ah, the punishment that will be meted out to them,' Mrs Roubínek sighed.

'Oh dear, that means Mr Vavřena will be in it too,' Lottie quavered.

'I can't understand why they won't let them have their innocent pleasures, I'm sure.'

'And there won't be any *Majales* either! I did so look forward to the festivities!' Lottie fretted and turned sad eyes on her new spring dress, which had been made specially for the occasion and was now prettily spread out on her bed.

Lenka, who had all this time been sitting in the front room, deeply engrossed in her book, was suddenly disturbed. The door opened quietly and, as she lowered her book, she had a pleasant shock of surprise — the same she had had once before. Vavřena bowed and, pointing to the door, asked quietly:

'Are they in there?'

'Yes, all of them are there.'

He unbuttoned his coat and took out a book which he

handed to Lenka with the words: 'This is serious reading.' Then he added with a smile: 'But I'll bring you something more entertaining on the first of May.'

Lenka glanced at the book's title.

'Would you like to become a philosopher?' Vavřena asked her softly. She blushed.

'Yes, if you'd help me.'

He pressed her hand hurriedly, knocked, and went next door. Lenka was in seventh heaven. She could not help hearing Lottie's cry of welcome, which would have made her unhappy at any other time, but now — Good Heavens! She looked at the title of the book, which read:

THE BRIDGE
Assorted Thoughts about Matters of Interest and
Importance to Everyone.
Compiled by M. F. KLÁCEL in his early
years for the younger generation.

While Lenka leafed through the book and sat once more lost in thought, Vavřena was under a crossfire. Mother and daughter, agog for news, plied him with questions, both wanting to know the real events of the fateful morning.

The student replied as best he could and smiled inwardly when a look of sympathy and assumed sadness spread over Lottie's face, while she asked with a coquettish air if he, too, would not be punished most severely.

'One for all and all for one, Miss Lottie,' came the swift reply.

'And what about the *Majales*?'

'There won't be any,' her mother answered, and Vavřena said nothing. This seemed to be a confirmation of Lottie's worst fears. Just then, however, the most extraordinary thing happened.

Mr Roubínek, sitting deep in thought at the other end of the room, had been trying to polish yet another sentence, without taking the slightest notice of anything or anyone in the room. Suddenly he put his quill down on the table and started to speak in his rasping, monotonous voice, while he looked at his beloved picture with a fish-like stare.

'Tutor, what's this I hear? What are these unheard of changes introduced into the Czech language?'

'At your service, sir.'

'I was on my way to church this morning, High Mass, you know, and I met a student — although who he was I couldn't say. He greeted me most politely, I will say that for him, but the way he said 'good morning' — well, I must say I was astounded!'

'I think I can explain that, sir. We don't use the German form of address any more, and to say just 'morning' is quite incorrect.'

Mr Roubínek's eyes wavered, left the picture, and settled strictly on the brave young man. For a second only, though, for they returned to the picture straight away, and Mr Roubínek held forth:

'What was good enough for my forefathers is good enough for me. Why, even men in high positions used the German form of address, and they knew what they were doing. As for what is correct and what is incorrect, I assure you we know as much about it as you do. Surely you acknowledge that Žižka and the Emperor Joseph were the best two Czechs that ever lived —' and with that he fell silent. His silence was full of meaning and Vavřena said nothing.

While Mrs Roubínek tried to steer the conversation into other channels, Vavřena, greatly amused though outwardly as serious as ever, silently finished Mr Roubínek's

38

sentence with 'our church is a memorial of them.' He got up and went to look for Fricek.

Mr Roubínek picked up his quill again, but found it difficult to continue with his letter.

Lottie folded up her new blue dress with a sigh and a heavy heart, and put it away in the big, old-fashioned wardrobe.

Without looking at anyone in particular, Mr Roubínek suddenely lifted his head and said:

'Another rebel with his stupid innovations!'

He seemed unable to recall his straying thoughts from his son's tutor.

4

The events of Sunday morning at the college of philosophy were something unheard of in the whole of Litomyšl. The town was seething with gossip and surmise and suggestions as to what would happen to the rebellious students. It was generally expected that exhaustive enquiries would start the very next day, and a few people even voiced the fear that some of the students would be victims of a *consilium abeundi*.

Contrary to all expections, however, it seemed as if the whole affair had been allowed to drop. It is true, the religious instructor did not put in an appearance the next day, but that was all.

'Oh well, there won't be any celebrations, even if the students are forgiven!'

'Litomyšl will never witness another *Majales*, what a dire thought!'

'Too true, more's the pity.'

Of all the people no one was more shocked than Miss Elis. Fear became her constant companion when she heard about the rioting, and she looked at her students with motherly reproach and compassion. At the same time she was greatly concerned about the good name of her flat. She was very proud of the fact that she had 'mothered' forty-seven students of philosophy of faultless reputation, who had achieved high marks in their studies. Some of them had later attained high positions, some had become priests, but one and all they kept in touch with her. What a dreadful thing that her students should be punished and, what was more, punished for insubordination!

On Monday morning, when all of them but Vavřena had left, she said dejectedly:

'Mr Vavřena, I haven't slept a wink all night. Is there any truth in what Mrs Řezničková has been telling me?'

'Dear me, what has she been telling you?'

'She said that you, Mr Vavřena, together with Mr Frybort were at the bottom of all the mischief.'

'My dear Miss Elis, please don't worry about that. That's nothing but malicious gossip, I assure you.'

'Oh, what a load off my mind! I thought so! How envious people are because of my flat! I said straight away, I told her: It might be true of all of them, but certainly not of my Mr Vavřena. It's true, Mr Frybort does fly off the handle occasionally, but this —'

'A lot is said with little truth in it.'

'There have been forty-seven students —' and she was about to continue what kind of students had lodged with her. But Vavřena picked up his hat and left.

Miss Elis's rooms were quiet and still. No one knew what a lot of things went on there under cover, least of all Miss Elis. Zelenka went about his business as usual, taking life as it came. He had not taken part in the students' riot, his conscience was completely clear; on the contrary, he felt annoyed at the thought that he too might be questioned. But apart from that, he gave his lessons, did his home-work and ate his meager rations of bread and fruit-stew.

Špína's horizon was still rather cloudy and he gave

41

vent to his feelings by smoking incessantly, concealing himself thereby behind a veritable smoke-screen. He had found a new job: he had unearthed in his wardrobe a black frock-coat which was an heirloom from his late uncle who had worn the garment as a student. Now Špína had the coat in front of him and sat looking at it for many minutes at a time. Every day, however, he would take it to the corridor, where he would brush it meticulously. He tried his hand as a tailor too.

Špína, while still a boy, used to spend his vacations with his uncle, whose habit it was to say: 'Sewing is an honourable trade, and 'tis a very poor student indeed who doesn't use a farthing's worth of thread every Sunday.' Now, years after the old man's demise, Špína tried to live up to his uncle's words and, although the effort was great, the success was small. Why this sudden concern about his looks? Why should a student, known for his rather cynical outlook, start to bother about his appearance? His secret was his own, but Miss Elis's guess was not far from the truth.

Another two days passed. Several students, Vavřena and Frybort among them, had to appear before the dean where they had to give an account of their actions during the riot. The dean informed them that the religious instructor would not enter the building again until proper apologies had been made.

The last day of April dawned before the matter could be settled.

It was late afternoon when Vavřena finished Fricek's lesson. He was about to leave, when Mrs Roubínek called him back.

'Oh, Mr Vavřena!'

He turned and came back.

'There was something I meant to tell you. Please don't use these new-fangled Czech words in my husband's

42

presence, or better still, speak German when he's here. He's so opposed to all the new expressions. *Er kann es nicht aussteheu.* He thinks it's done on purpose to annoy him.'

A deep red began to spread across Vavřena's face. He smiled and bowed without a word, and left. His retort would have been a biting one.

His anger faded at the sight of Lenka, whom he met in the corridor. Her eyes, too, lit up when she came face to face with him.

'Mistress Lenka, may I tell you something in confidence?' he asked hurriedly and, having made certain that they were unobserved, he bent towards her and whispered into her ear. When Lenka straightened up again she was alone, except for the quick steps on the stairs.

She stood motionless for a moment, her eyes fixed on the door as if expecting an explanation. But the steps faded into utter silence and, pulling herself back to the present, Lenka slipped into her room with the graceful movement of a gazelle.

She felt elated and happy beyond words.

Špína's life had been nice and pleasant while his uncle had been alive. When he died, Špína, who had no parents and who was without friends or money, had to earn his living by giving private lessons. Just now he had returned from another such lesson and was about to light his pipe because he intended to smoke while reading, when he stopped in his tracks as though frozen to the spot. His knees trembled violently, he was unable to move or to utter a sound.

He stood at the half-open door, looking into Miss Elis's room through the gap. The sound of a clear high voice, which affected him so strongly, came from the other room.

He caught sight of Márinka, who was the very picture of health and bubbling gaiety. Although she was dressed simply, her white apron, short skirt and low shoes enhanced her prettiness even more.

'I won't stay long, I only came for a little chat. Are your boarders in?'

'No, I'm afraid they're out teaching,' Miss Elis said, unaware that Špína had returned.

'I had to come. You know, Miss Elis, I thought that perhaps you would know a little more than I.'

'What is it that you'd like to know, my dear?'

'There's a rumour in the town that the *Majales* will be held this year. Have you heard anything about it? Wouldn't it be glorious if it were true?'

Špína, watching her intently, noticed her lively manner, her joyful movements, her dancing, shining eyes. Oh, how adorable she was!

The occasion for which he had prayed and hoped for oh! so long had come at last, and all he had to do now was enter the room and tell her what he knew. How grateful she would be to him! But there was nothing he could do to overcome his shyness, and although he would have dearly liked to talk to her, he would not have known what to say. She was so gay, so high-spirited and alive, and what would happen if she teased him? The times he had stopped, determined he would speak to her, his lips had even shaped the words he was about to say, but at the last moment he had kept silent. Now he had his chance, and what a chance! She wanted to know something he could tell her, all he had to do was go next door and answer her — his heart beat madly against his ribs. Oh Lord, help me, stand by me, give me strength to go in and talk to her. There has to be a first time for everything, a little while yet, I'll let Miss Elis answer her, and then —

44

'My dear child, I'm so sorry I must dash your hopes, the students rioted the other day, and I don't think we'll hear any more about the *Majales*.'

Špína took a deep breath — his hand was on the door-knob, this time he would go up and speak to her. But the door leading into the corridor opened and Frybort — the insolence and arrogance of him! — came into the room. Špína had lost his case even before he had started to defend it.

Slowly he took his hand off the door. His self-confidence had vanished, gone were his resolutions; he dare not brave comparison, for he knew he would be second-best. His heart filled with bitterness and envy. He had not moved away from the door, he stood quite still and watched Márinka and saw her start and blush at Frybort's unexpected entry.

'Oh Mr Frybort, I'm so glad you've come,' Miss Elis said and explained Márinka's mission in a few words.

'Well, to tell the truth, the festival is not supposed to be held this year, but since it is your express wish we'll celebrate it as whole-heartedly as we used to in the past.'

'I'd like to know if you're as almighty as you seem to think.'

'Don't you believe me? Would you like to take a bet on it?'

'All right. If you lose I'll give you a bunch of stinging-nettles.'

'And if I win, I'll get a bunch of violets. A nice little bunch, you know like the one —' his eyes were full of meaning.

'Very well, a bunch of flowers then,' Márinka cut him short, while she looked at Miss Elis shyly.

Špína was on tenterhooks. Why could not he ever think of such things to say! He was pleased to see that

45

Márinka was suddenly saying good-bye lightly and that she hurried from the room. Her mother's voice, calling her, was distinctly audible.

When Frybort entered his room a little later, he bumped into Špína, who was in a hurry to be off.

'What's the rush?'

An indistinct murmur was all the answer he got.

Dusk settled over the countryside - it was the eve of the first of May.

The air was pleasant, although the sky was dark and starless. The hills and woods and dales and brooks, the whole countryside was shrouded in a screen of mist, over which a number of bonfires threw their bright light. Young and old alike strolled towards the fires, eager to see 'the burning of the witches' and to spend a nice evening. The largest crowd had gathered around the statue of St Procopius, which stood on a little hill, where the foliage of bushy linden-trees rustled gently above people's heads.

A little further a big bonfire had been lit, and exuberant youngsters ran around it, shouting and calling to each other, throwing burning brooms high up into the air. Sparks flying off the burning brooms were accompanied by shouts of approval and cheering.

Vavřena stood apart from the crowd, half turned away from the fire. He did not join any of the groups which stood around the fire, for he wanted, above all, to be alone.

His thoughts were far away, his eyes wandered towards the woods, which seemed secretive and silent in the evening dusk. The lake shone like a mirror in the valley, untouched by the shadows of the trees so high above it. The walls of the Manor house stood out whitely through the trees like the ruins of an ancient castle.

As far as the eye could reach, on all the hills surround-

46

ing the countryside, fires threw their bright glow into the night.

The evening with its fires, with its shouts of delight and irregular lights strewn here and there, the whole atmosphere turned Vavřena's thoughts towards his home and, still more, towards his boyhood. His memory brought back the times when he had lit just such fires and jumped across their blaze; numerous other pictures stood out in his mind and changed with great speed.

Suddenly a voice spoke not far away from him: 'I can't imagine what they see in it.' And another voice joined in:

'*Ach, das gemeine Volk!*'

He recognized Mrs Roubínek and Miss Lottie by their remarks. He had no wish to meet them here and so, without turning round, he walked away and instinctively turned towards the ridge between the fields. The ladies passed and, as he walked on, the noise receded until at last it became nothing but a faint murmur coming through the night.

Vavřena was carried away by his thoughts. A soothing breath of air cooled his brow and brought to his nostrils the scent of green corn, and the dewy grass felt like a silky carpet under his feet.

Now, under the silent, endless sky his thoughts wandered away from home, back to the present, to Lenka, to what the evening might have been like, had she come to the fire too.

He mused and imagined that he was walking side by side with her, he conversed tenderly with her and confided in her, and she answered him as indeed she would have done, had she been there in reality.

Suddenly he collided with somebody, somebody as far away in thought as he himself.

47

'Good Lord, Špína, is that you? What on earth —'

His friend, however, caught his hand and looked at him. He seemed distraught, excited, and spoke with difficulty.

'Old man, I've got to, I mean I must ... I ... I ... oh, darn it, no, I won't!' And with that he was gone.

When Vavřena turned round he saw him stalking towards the town.

5

The crowds dispersed, the noise diminished, the fires turned into an ever-dwindling glow until that, too, died down. The cloak of night made shadows of the trees, with a glow of fire showing here and there, and as time went on and hour after hour passed, these glows became extinguished too, and complete darkness enfolded the whole countryside. No sound came from anywhere, silence and darkness, the majesty of night reigned supreme.

No human eye has ever seen nature awaken from her slumbers, and yet, you sense the change, the coming back to life. Your heart melts within you and your mind produces fragrant dreams and you are full of understanding for the purity of nature. The murmur of the brook has ceased to be a mystery to you, the trembling of young beeches is full of meaning.

Your dreams, so frail and tender, walk ahead of you under a starlit sky. They barely touch the trees and gardens, but go on until they come to rooms and garrets. All nature is in bloom as if touched by quiet drops of dew.

Night passes and there, beyond the woods the first rays appear, heralding the birth of a new day, the first day of the month of May. The nymphs, realizing their

49

time is short, follow night's shadows deep into the woods.

A quivering stream of golden light crosses the sky; night flees, carrying off all dreams, and a new day dawns.

Lenka's dreams flew out of her window on rose-coloured wings.

She awoke and lay still, looking about with unseeing eyes, spellbound by her lovely dream. Suddenly her attention was arrested by the trees outside her window and she skipped out of bed as nimbly as a bird. A miracle had happened overnight, the trees had been transformed: every crown, every branch had changed into a mass of white blossoms. She opened her window wide, and looked out with mingled wonder and delight. It was bright daylight, although the sun was invisible still. The morning air blew freshly against Lenka's cheeks and hark! there was the sound of music carried on unseen wings from the town-square. Thus the celebrations of the first day of the glorious month of hawthorn blossom started.

A tremor of happiness passed through Lenka as the hushed music came to her ears. Vavřena's whispered words were firmly imprinted upon her memory, they were no dream, they were true! True!

The music swelled and came nearer until it finally reached a crescendo under the Manor. The sun had risen meanwhile and Lenka's room was filled with a golden light.

Mr Roubínek, his white night-cap still perched on his head, was putting on his coloured dressing-gown, the Colonel, which he had inherited from his uncle.

He crossed the room and stood at the window, from where he watched the band which had arrived at the old manor-house and struck up their serenade. All members of the band were in the uniform of the town's sharpshooter regiment.

Lottie, dressed in a snow-white negligé, appeared

behind her father, while Lenka who was fully dressed went about her household duties with a happy smile on her lips.

Few people slept late that morning. Those who had not got up to go out, leaned out of their windows to see the radiant sky or to watch the band, whose music rose to a tremendous pitch one moment, only to disappear and start up again at another end of the town.

Špína, however, slept like a log. Miss Elis was more than surprised that he had come home so late at night. Vavřena had left early in the morning, Zelenka had followed on his heels, carrying a book under his arm.

At breakfast time Miss Elis opened the door to the students' room quietly to see if Frybort was still asleep, and was surprised to find him fully dressed, walking up and down and — reading! Wonders never cease, she thought. Or had something happened to him?

When Miss Elis was alone at last she went into her lodgers' room to dust and tidy up in general. There was a small book on the edge of the table which she recognized immediately, for it was the book which Frybort had been studying with such interest earlier on. Surely there must be a spell on it since it had held his attention so completely! Miss Elis opened it where the mark had been placed, and read:

The Tipsy Miller.

'*Stop shouting at me, dear wife, do*
Stop nagging at me like a shrew,'
The miller told his mate;
'*You act as if I'd taken a girl for a walk*
Or caused some other kind of talk
And all because of my tipsy state.'

51

What a poem, Miss Elis thought, goodness, what a poem! Trust the students to get hold of something like this. Whatever could the book be called? Miss Elis read the same title which Vavřena had read to Lenka. She was about to shut the book when she noticed an inscription on the fly-leaf. She stood quite still for a few seconds, then she read and re-read the inscription again, whereupon she took the book to the window and gave the handwriting a minute scrutiny. Deep emotion showed on her tired, lined face. She stood there, lost in thought and then, suddenly, she went to her room and, opening the closet, took out her prayer-books.

There was a gilt-edged leaf in one of them, yellow with age, which had obviously been torn out of a poetry-album.

A picture in water-colours was painted on the leaf, showing a white birch-tree whose long, slender branches just touched a tomb stone. Tree and stone were overgrown with ivy. They stood on the shores of a lake, on the other side of which there were dense woods. It was sun-down and the last rays just touched the sky. The other side of the leaf bore an inscription:

> Behold this grave embedded in fresh grass,
> It lies low, so low;
> It holds my life and happiness and woe
> And your bitter tears, sweet lass.

The writing on the leaf and in the book was identical. Miss Elis could read no further, the leaf fluttered from her hand. It fell on the book, whose title signed 'Myslimír' drew her eyes again and again. Tears filled her eyes and she turned her head away; her glance fell on the picture showing the young priest, adorned by a half-wreath of

52

artificial flowers. Miss Elis folded her wrinkled, old hands in an involuntary gesture.

Frybort came rushing home after eleven o'clock and hurried to his room. Miss Elis, however, stopped him immediately and questioned him about the book. She was told that it was Vavřena's. And when Vavřena came home soon after, he was very surprised at Miss Elis's question.

'Oh please, do tell me. You don't know how much it means to me,' she pleaded and her kind, faded eyes looked at him beseechingly. He told her that the book belonged to Lenka.

'I've heard about her, and I've even seen her twice. I know she doesn't go out much and I, at my age, go out even less.'

Vavřena's surprise grew.

'She's kind and good I've heard, but I'm sure her life is none too easy.'

'Would you like to meet her?'

'Oh, do you think I could?'

'There's nothing easier than that. Today, if you like!'

'Do you mean that, really and truly?'

'Could we have our lunch, Miss Elis?' Frybort called from the other room. 'We're in rather a hurry.'

The lovely morning had turned into a really warm day. Church bells pealed, announcing mid-day, and Mr Roubínek was in the middle of his lunch, which he enjoyed tremendously. Lottie was unusually quiet and, as Lenka never had much to say, Mrs Roubínek's flow of words was almost uninterrupted; Lenka had to leave the table at frequent intervals to see to the food. The morning's happy mood still showed on her features and every time she passed the window she looked out towards the Piarist college. Gone was her serious expression, a smile played on her lips more than once, while her aunt held forth on the feeling of excitement the first of May evoked, and went on to say that she had noticed how restless the students had become.

'That's probably because of the interdiction,' Lottie said. 'Can you wonder at them?'

Mr Roubínek paid little enough attention to the talk. However, suddenly he stiffened, his fork stayed in mid air and his eyes, fixed as usual on King Herod, wavered and turned in amazement to his wife and daughter. The eyes of the three met in surprise, whereupon Lottie jumped up from her chair and made for the window.

'Music, it's really music,' she exclaimed excitedly, but she calmed down again after a little.

'What's this? Music at midday? I've never heard of such a thing.' Mr Roubínek was astonished.

'Why, of course you have. Don't you remember, when the *Majales* —' his daughter started again.

But her mother cut her short. 'Could they possibly —' and then she, too, went to the window while Fricek, making the most of his opportunity, threw down his fork, got off his chair and ran out of the house and down the street for all he was worth.

He was gone before his father's reproving voice could reach him.

The music, faint at first, grew in volume until it reached a crescendo near the college; the hill between the Manor, the college and the grammar school was soon crammed with people, most of whom were students.

The astonishment of Mr Roubínek and of all his family, except Lenka, knew no bounds. Lenka had been told about the plan beforehand. While they were all standing about, voicing their surprise, Vavřena entered the room. He bowed to the ladies and, telling them that May Day would be celebrated in the traditional manner,

54

invited them to join in the festivities. The students' parade was to start at any minute, complete with brass-band, and they'd all march to the Nedošín woods, as they had done in previous years. He was gone again before Mrs Roubínek had time to ask for explanations.

Lottie was elated. She hurried to the wardrobe and lovingly took out her pretty new spring dress.

'Let's hurry, mamma, I don't want to be late. Do hurry, please!'

'Not so fast, my dear, not so fast. Goodness knows what's at the back of it all,' her father remarked.

'Oh, don't spoil the child's simple pleasure. I'm sure the students got permission at the last moment,' Mrs Roubínek said.

The crowds in the streets grew denser, the noise increased. The band stopped playing as the air was rent by a shout which sounded like a volley of rifle shots:

'*Vivat academia!*'

The band played the fanfare.

'*Vivant professores!*' hundreds of young voices shouted and the band repeated the fanfare.

'*Vivant professores!*' Mr Roubínek repeated to himself as he nodded his head in satisfaction.

His household was thrown into happy confusion. A strange thing happened, though. Lenka helped them all, she was here, there and everywhere, and yet when the time came she, too, was prepared. She did not go out with her aunt as a rule, not even when she was asked to, but today this 'stubborn creature', as her aunt called her on the side, wanted to go with them to the woods!

Mrs Roubínek's eyes questioned her husband's face.

'Oh well, let her come, she can look after Fricek at the same time. I don't think either of them has had a chance to watch the comedy before.'

Having had his say, Mr Roubínek took no more notice of them. He sat in his easy-chair, smoked and fixed his eyes on the picture of King Herod.

Father Germanus, the professor of history at the College, walked along the corridor, where he met the religious instructor, who looked deathly pale.

'I presume you've seen and heard what's going on,' asked the latter in a trembling voice.

'Of course I have. Did you hear this now?' Father Germanus replied with a smile.

'*Vivant professores!*' voices thundered outside.

'Why, this is unheard of! *Coniuratio!*'

'*Secessio!*' the old man chuckled. 'History teaches us in theory what you see here in practice, only on a much smaller scale ot course. Suppressed freedom, privileges —'

'A stop must be put to it at once. I'm going to see the dean about it.'

'I'll come with you then.'

The infuriated priest entered the room, with Father Germanus in his wake. The dean, having pushed aside some of the instruments on the table, stood at the window, watching the crowds outside.

'What are they doing now?' wailed the religious instructor.

'Restless young blood is making itself felt, that's all.'

'Well, have the goodness to tell them to disperse.'

'I don't think they would disperse, even if I were to tell them to. Since they were bold enough for this —'

'But this! It must be broken up, I tell you.'

'Broken up? By whom, pray? Kmoníček?' Father Germanus smiled again gently.

'All right, I'll tell them myself to disperse quietly.'

56

'Very well, you may do so in my name,' the dean replied. The minister left the room.

In the meantime the students had lined up in full strength. It was a pleasant sight to watch the youths, to see them fall in line swinging their philosophers' canes. The multitude of voices, the calling and the shouting and, above all, the laughter and the *badinage!*

People thronged around the students, all faces showing approval and good humour. Only a few of the surprised townsmen voiced their objections to the celebration. The band, quiet for a while, started up in full just as the religious instructor reached the bottom of the stairs. The musicians marched off, and the students fell into step behind them.

The street resounded with the pounding of hundreds of marching feet. The crowds pushed and shoved, and all those who had time followed the students; all over town people came out of their houses to see if there was truth in what was being said, and as they saw the oncoming parade they rushed inside again to prepare for the celebration in the woods. Almost the whole of Litomyšl was used to taking part in the festivities in the Nedošín woods.

The students had moved off, the music was but a faraway, blurred sound. The religious instructor stood there, alone, humiliated and enraged. As long as he could remember, nay, even longer, such a thing had never happened yet.

The conspiracy had succeeded. Beyond a doubt, the students were all for one and one for all, without a word endangering their cause.

The town was buzzing with activity. The unexpected, the long-awaited, longed-for holiday, crossed off the Litomyšl calendar three years ago, had come.

People left their houses and one and all they made for the woods. Here was a settled citizen with his whole family, there again a mother with her daughters. Some came singly, others were in groups. All of them without exception spoke of the surprising turn of events, for none of them had expected it and because of that they welcomed it all the more.

It was with something of a shock that Miss Elis listened to Frybort's last minute invitation. She hesitated and said she would not come, but when Vavřena whispered that she would see Lenka there she changed her mind at once.

The good lady started to dress as soon as she was alone. Her clothes were the same as those she had worn in her youth; long gloves, reaching high up above her wrists, a narrow cloak made of pure silk were the last garments she donned. Márinka's mother came in when Miss Elis was fully dressed and ready to leave.

'Oh, I'm so glad, Miss Elis, that you intend to go. My girl is almost in tears, she wants to go so badly. I expect she thinks it wouldn't be complete without her. I can't shut up shop because of the festival, can I now. If at least my husband was at home, but there's nothing I can do as things are now.'

'Do let Márinka come, I'd be delighted to take her under my wing, if you'd let me,' Miss Elis cut her short.

'How kind of you, Miss Elis, she'll be awfully pleased. And you won't have to wait for her, I'll be bound; when it's a question of fun or entertainment these girls can get dressed quicker than you'd think.'

'I'm not surprised. After all, we're young only once in our lives.'

Oh, woods of Nedošín, your glory has passed long since. Your trees have lost their denseness, gone are your

58

pavilions and alcoves. Where is your entertainment hall, witnessing youth's revelries and dances!

But at the time of our story the woods were at the height of their glory.

The paths leading to the woods and to the pond were alive with people. Beyond the pond dense trees displayed their freshly-green splendour. A wooded hill rose steeply above the forest and green tree tops peeped from behind its crest. Today the hum of merry voices, laughter, shouting, music and singing seemed to have made nature part of all the gaiety.

Gay music could be heard from far away, and when it fell silent exuberant voices, joined in song, came from within the depths of the forest.

> *In silvis resonant*
> *dulcia carmina,*
> *in silvis resonat*
> *dulce carmen!*

No sooner had the choir finished, there came — as if in answer to the song — another group of voices from quite a different part:

> *Dulcia carmina*
> *in silvis resonant,*
> *in silvis resonat*
> *dulce carmen —*

The woods were crowded when Miss Elis and Márinka arrived. A nice, fair-sized house with an arcade, which was the restaurant, stood well inside the forest. There were rough wooden planks serving as benches in front of it, and the guests sat either on those, or on the smooth green grass under the shady trees. Laughter and light-hearted talk filled the air. The centre of the festivities, however, was the entertainment hall, which was at the top of the hill; the footpath leading there, past St Antony's Chapel, was filled to overflowing.

A sun-filled, golden light filtered through the tree tops outlining gaily attired people against the green foliage of May.

Márinka could hardly curb her impatience. Her young eyes scanned the faces of the people and came to rest on a group of students who were busy with their drinks. Miss Elis too watched everything with interest. Suddenly they came to a halt. Mrs Roubínek and Lottie were coming towards them.

'She didn't take her ward with her, I notice,' Márinka commented.

'Oh, they never take the poor child anywhere. I'm sure she doesn't even know about this.'

A few steps further Márinka turned off the path and they walked deeper into the woods.

'Oh look, there's somebody reciting over there. It's Mr Frybort, I do believe! Let's go over and listen to him, shall we?'

'All right, if you like.'

They came to a large group of people, in the centre of which Frybort stood on an old tree stump, reciting the poem Miss Elis readily recognized as the one Frybort had studied early in the morning. It was the poem about the tipsy miller. Frybort's audience listened eagerly, and shouts of laughter brought forth by the witty poem as well as by its excellent recital, were his reward.

Márinka's eyes never once left his face; he jumped off the stump as soon as the recital was over and came towards her.

He welcomed them both heartily and, on hearing where Márinka wanted to go, led them out of the forest onto a path passing the grotto-like Chapel, beneath which there bubbled a little brook. They came upon the entertainment hall suddenly, without warning. The hall consisted of a light roof which rested on four tree-trunks, and a flat, bare floor. In spite of its obvious plainness the hall was crowded with eager dancers.

The band, placed a little to the side, was playing a polka. Miss Elis found herself alone before she had even looked around properly. Márinka looked entranced as Frybort led her to the floor, and thereafter Miss Elis only got a glimpse of her head, bobbing up and down among the other couples.

Even more people had drifted over to watch the dancers.

Miss Elis thought she might find Vavřena here, but saw no sign of him at all. She had asked Frybort about him and had been told that Vavřena was with Mrs Roubínek and Lottie. Lottie, however, was among the dancers now, and Vavřena was not her partner.

After a little, Miss Elis left the crush of people, for she needed a rest. She walked away and found herself in a rather lonely spot, where even the sounds of music reached her only faintly. She stood and sighed. She felt relieved, but a strange uneasiness assailed her at the same time.

A gay tune came faintly to her ears, and it sounded like the echo of times gone by — her own happy youth. She stood there, dreaming, and everything reminded her of it, the gorgeous day, the shady trees, unchanged and unchanging, the noise and shouts and merry-making, the festivities as they had always been: the difference lay only in the faces.

61

Her mind was busy, remembering dear faces, one of which stood out very clearly. It was the face of a tall youth, whom she was walking arm in arm with, away from the dancers, towards the woods. She was listening to him, drinking in every word he said. Her memory brought back other happy pictures too, and passed them and came to the final painful one: the heart-breaking scene of leave-taking, their desperate parting from each other, here in these woods, almost in the very spot. He had sacrificed himself as well as her to his parents' will.

In the depths of the woods there stood an old old gnarled tree, with no thought of attracting anyone's attention and yet, the unexpected happened.

Lenka, upon leaving her noisy companions, looked around for Miss Elis about whom Vavřena had told her as soon as he had welcomed Mrs Roubínek. She wandered off and came to the old tree. She liked the secluded, shaded spot — it was such ages since she had been to the woods last in spite of her great love for them. She had spent her childhood in a region rich with forests, where she had romped and roamed alone or walked sedately with her uncle.

Now, after a time which seemed longer than it was, once more she heard the tree tops murmur high up above her head, once more she felt the smooth breath of the trees; she stayed there under the old tree, feeling happy and secure. Her trained eye had found something which kept her rooted to the spot: a huge branch grew out of the old tree-trunk high above the ground and there, right in the corner of trunk and branch, there was a bird's nest as if glued to them.

At that moment Vavřena too found the secluded spot, or rather that which he was looking for.

Stepping out from the under-growth he saw Lenka looking upwards, watching the tree-trunk intently. Now she stood on her toes and looked and looked —

She wore a light-blue dress and looked fresh and slim and flushed. Oh, how pretty she seemed to Vavřena!

She walked towards the tree on tip-toe, when suddenly startled, she turned round. Although the colour heightened in her cheeks, she put her finger to her lips and bade him to be quiet. He, in turn, tiptoed up to Lenka and looked up at the bird's nest.

'Do you see it?' Lenka asked in whispers.

'No, I'm afraid I don't.'

'You must look over here. See the tiny beak, the head and those little black eyes?'

'Oh yes, I see it now.' He looked intently at the little bird, whose small head protruded beyond the nest. They stood there next to each other and Vavřena felt his pulses quicken, the blood rushed to his face. Two hearts talked to each other in the silence and it seemed incredible that their voices were inaudible.

The student turned away from the nest and his head began to swim as his eyes met Lenka's. Her eyes seemed to be liquid in their beauty, and she seemed to smile at him not only with her lips, but with her eyes and with her heart as well.

'Let's leave the birds, shall we? We might frighten them,' she said as if talking in a dream.

He did as he was bid and they left the tree, hand in hand like children. They walked along the winding, grassy path, and sunshine and cool shade alternated in quick succession; the strains of a merry tune came softly to their ears.

Suddenly Lenka pulled her hand away and peered ahead. An elderly lady stood not far away, dressed unfashionably in a large hat, a narrow cloak, and long gloves which reached high above her elbows.

'Why, that's Miss Elis,' Vavřena exclaimed.

They made friends in a little while, and sat down on a near-by wooden bench beneath an old, old tree. Soon they were on common ground.

Miss Elis told Lenka that she had been wanting to meet her for a very long time. Although as a rule she never went to parties and suchlike, today she had made a point of walking all this distance for one reason only: to meet her and to discuss the almanac she had seen in Vavřena's possession. Dropping her eyes, she asked:

'Those verses on the fly-leaf: were they written by a priest?'

'Yes,' Lenka answered, 'my uncle wrote them.'

Silence fell between them.

The music started up again just then, and Vavřena listened to it, slightly startled. His face clouded.

'Oh dear, that seems to be the quadrille and I was to be Miss Lottie's partner!'

'Then you must keep your word.' Miss Elis urged him to be gone.

'It irks me, but I suppose I'll have to. You will wait here for me, won't you?'

'If Mistress Lenka will —'

'Gladly,' she said bestowing a sweet smile on him and he, bowing to the ladies, disappeared through the shrubs.

Some time passed again in silence, then Lenka resumed the conversation shyly. 'You weren't altogether a stranger to me, Miss Elis. You see —'

'You knew me? From your uncle?' Miss Elis asked.

'Yes. You see, my uncle had a picture made in tapestry, and I think — I thought — it was from you, wasn't it?'

'Yes. It was Faith, Hope and Charity,' Miss Elis sighed.

'That's right. My uncle was very attached to it. I found a date and your name marked on it and I rather thought it was dear to him, a memory of something that had happened in his youth. And then, I also found a — a note from you in a Czech book.'

The present faded, their thoughts flew back into the past, to times far happier than the present ones. The years fell away from Miss Elis as she sat there listening to Lenka. Her hands lay folded in her lap, her head was bent, and often she would sigh and glance at Lenka's face. Slowly her heart, so filled with sweetly bitter memories, tore down the defences built around it and, as she began to tell her story, haltingly at first, Miss Elis felt released as if from a heavy load.

Lenka's uncle, Father George, had been born in Litomyšl. He was distantly related to Miss Elis, whom he had fallen in love with while studying philosophy. She returned his feelings with all the fervour of her youth and so, for a time, the two young people were secretly, glowingly happy.

'But his mother — your grandmother — was a very pious woman. While George was still a child she pledged him to become a priest,' Miss Elis continued, having explained the family connections.

'During his term of physics he told his mother he did not want to take the Cloth, but she cried and wept and pleaded with him and finally, when he was adamant, she fell very ill. It almost broke her heart that her pledge to God was to stay unfulfilled. Things came to a head and George's father fell on his knees before his son, and so — well — what more is there to tell! George was to leave after vacations to enter the Seminary. He said, before he left,

65

he wanted to talk to me; we met here, in these woods, almost at this very spot and here — here we said good-bye for ever.'

Miss Elis was too overcome with emotion to continue. Her kind, blue eyes were brimming with tears.

'And you never saw him any more?' Lenka asked quietly, for she too was deeply moved.

'Oh yes, I saw him again. When your grandmother got well again, she invited me to accompany her and your grandfather, when they went to Prague on St John's Day, to visit George. Oh, I didn't want to go, and yet how I longed to at the same time. But be that as it may, I couldn't turn down their invitation, my parents insisted. And so I went along. Arrived in Prague, I got separated from your grandfather in the crowded streets. I walked about aimlessly, until I came upon an old gentleman in shining, high boots. He reminded me so much of our deacon, I did not feel afraid of him. He was a priest, you see. I walked up to him and kissed his hand and asked him if he could tell me where the seminary was. I thought I'd meet your grandparents there again. He smiled at me with so much kindness and asked if I had a brother there, and I — God knows how I felt. At any rate, he led me to a big black building and said: 'Go through the gate and then across the court-yard to the left, and you'll find the seminary. There's a gatekeeper there and you can ask your way about.' I thanked him and walked on. It was late afternoon by then and the tall dark buildings cast a gloomy shadow on my path. There were very few people about; when I had nearly reached my destination I saw a young priest of similar height and build as George. Believe me, a pang went through my heart when I saw the cassock.

' "That's what George wears too" I thought and tears

66

welled up in my eyes. Dear God, I shall never forget that moment. He came towards me and my knees trembled as I recognized him, for it was George, but he was different, so pale and thin. I started to cry when I saw the change in him, nothing else mattered, not even the surroundings. I caught hold of his hand as if to prevent his flight and he stood over me and soothed me and tried to calm me down, while his own voice shook uncontrollably, poor lamb. Thus his parents found us. What a good thing, it was almost dark by then. What with the dusk and their own happiness they failed to notice my tear-stained face. We stayed in Prague for two whole days and George accompanied us everywhere. I, however, saw nothing of the beauties of the town, I was deaf and blind to everything but George, and so when I came home at last, there was little I could tell them.'

Miss Elis fell silent again.

A mild breeze blew across the trees and brought with it faint sounds of the quadrille.

'He used to come home for vacations,' Miss Elis continued, 'but I hardly ever spoke to him. I tried to avoid him whenever I could; I meant it for his own good, you know, but it was cruelly difficult for me. And no one knew, no one had an inkling. He wrote to me before he was ordained, and sent me a note for my album. It was the writing on the note that made me recognize the writing in the book, your book that is. He served his first High Mass here, in Dean Church. I was there too, I had to go, you see. People would have wondered otherwise. At any rate, when I saw him in his surplice near the altar I felt giddy and faint and had to leave the church. I was ill for a long, long time afterwards. How gladly I'd have died then.'

The silence was undisturbed. Miss Elis had finished

67

her tale and Lenka was too moved to say anything. The old lady's heart felt sore and yet relieved, for surely, surely there was not a more fitting recipient of her confidence than this soft-hearted child who had loved the priest so dearly.

'What's past is past,' Miss Elis said after a little while, and a sad smile played on her lips. 'Your fate will be different from mine, my dear, I'm sure of that,' she added, and Lenka, looking up at her dropped her eyes again, for Vavřena was hurrying towards them.

'He will never be a priest,' Miss Elis whispered hastily into her neighbour's ear.

'Why, Mr Vavřena, the quadrille isn't over yet! The band is still playing!'

'I'm afraid I've had some bad luck, Miss Elis. I hurried away from here to take my place with the other dancers, and I would have been on time if I hadn't had the ill fortune to meet the Roller woman on the way. You know what she's like, she stopped me and talked to me and I just couldn't get away. In the end I just apologized and ran. But when I came to the hall it was too late. The dance had begun and Lottie sat by her mother's side, on the far side of the hall.'

'Oh my goodness, Mr Vavřena!' Miss Elis said apprehensively.

'That'll cause quite a storm, I'm afraid,' Lenka sighed.

'Oh, as for the storm, that's broken already. I went over to apologize, Miss Lottie sat there like a thunder-cloud and Mrs Roubínek gave me the sharp side of her tongue.'

'I can well believe that. But you really ought to make it up with them, you know, just to be on the safe side,' Miss Elis admonished.

'Oh, it's all my fault, I kept you!' Lenka looked

troubled, but Vavřena waved his hand resolutely and said lightly:

'What's done is done. There's no need to be afraid. I'd like to stay here with you, if you'll let me; it's so nice and restful.'

'I'm worried about Fricek, Mr Vavřena.'

'Unnecessarily, I assure you. He's safe and sound and in good hands.'

'But what will happen, if Auntie is really cross with you?'

'And if she discharges you,' Miss Elis added.

The two young people looked at each other at these words, and the same unpleasant thought crossed both their minds: they would have no chance of meeting daily.

However, Vavřena shook his head energetically.

'I don't think that's likely to happen.'

Suddenly there was a movement in the near-by shrubs, and leaves and twigs rustled as they were being pushed aside.

'Good heavens, it seems we're in for it again. The hawk is about to swoop down on us,' Vavřena remarked as the eyes of all three turned towards the shrubs, where a small elderly woman appeared. She was neither fat nor thin, and her most remarkable feature were her eyes, which were small and beady and seemed to take everything in at a glance.

Her left hand gripped her inevitable knitting-bag, containing a ball of wool, knitting needles and a stocking. Her eyes swept over the little group under the tree, whereupon a peculiar smile twisted her lips.

'Ah, the diligent student, if my poor eyes do not deceive me. Is the quadrille over yet?' She spoke in German. 'My, my, and we were in such a hurry to be gone, weren't we! Oh, and Miss Elis is here too! I wish you a very good day.'

69

Throwing a glance full of malevolence in their direction she said good day again sarcastically and walked off without waiting for a reply.

Vavřena made a violent movement, but Miss Elis caught his hand and Lenka, who had kept her eyes averted in order to escape Mrs Roller's venomous glance, looked up entreatingly.

'The old busybody, the mean gossip! I should have given her a piece of my mind! She thinks she's still the mayor's wife, so that she can make everybody's life a misery and boss and bully people as she used to while her husband was alive.'

'You know what she's like, Mr Vavřena, no good would come of it if you were to answer back,' Miss Elis tried to soothe him.

'Of course I know what she's like; she's a scandal-monger who wags her tongue all day. You know her as well as I do, don't you? She's neither Czech nor German and you told me yourself how she hounded the late Mrs Rettig!'

'I know all that. But Mistress Lenka —' Miss Elis interrupted the flow of words.

'Ah yes, I'd forgotten she visits Mrs Roubínek sometimes,' Vavřena said more calmly. Poor Lenka, she should not suffer through any act of his.

'She does visit us occasionally and I know a lot about her through other people's talk. But I don't care if she comes and tells on me, really I don't. I don't know about you, though.' She smiled and her eyes, turned on Vavřena, finished the sentence for her. 'But now I'll have to leave.'

'We'll come with you, shall we?' Miss Elis rose.

Vavřena, turning as if by accident, looked at the old tree again. Suddenly he cried:

'Oh look, Mistress Lenka, the little bird has left its nest!'

70

'While we were sitting on the bench I thought how awful it would be if there were a strong wind or a thunderstorm. The whole nest might be destroyed.'

'We'll wait a while and I'll tell you in a few days' time if anything has changed in this beautiful spot.'

'It seems I'll keep you busy! I can't get over *The Bridge* which you lent me, either. There's a lot I don't understand about it. I must say I find it most difficult to become a philosopher.'

'Oh, I'll gladly lend you a helping hand with that. And I've brought you —'

'You haven't forgotten? You've brought me the book you promised me!'

Vavřena took a small, thin book from his pocket. 'Have a look at it while I fetch Fricek.' With that he hurried off. Lenka opened the book, full of curiosity. The first lines read:

'Twas twilight — and the first of May
May's evening — was the time of love —'

6

The Nedošín woods were full of gaiety and song and laughter. The densest crowds had collected outside the dance hall and a little lower down where the restaurant stood. The footpaths too, were full of people, most of them young.

Deep within the woods on a quiet path, Špína walked sedately, deep in thought. He was dressed up in his frock-coat, the very one he had inherited from his uncle. He had brushed and cleaned it meticulously in preparation for this event; a well-preserved castor adorned his head. His mind, fighting a losing battle with his shyness, was full of Márinka, whom he had seen among the dancers, looking radiant and glowing. He felt a devouring fire consuming him.

Oh, how he yearned to dance with her, to hold her close to his heart! He had watched her, longing to take her in his arms, and while he was trying to make up his mind — he knew he was no great light as a dancing partner — she had slipped away, unnoticed by him. He looked for her and decided that he would ask her for a dance, in spite of everything. He wondered how to address her, how to ask her, he even tried a formal little bow, when suddenly his mind was brought back with a start.

72

He heard dim voices from beyond the bushes and he listened to what they said.

'I've won the flowers, haven't I? The same ones as on the stairs?'

'Yes. Here they are. Are you satisfied now?'

'And I'll give you this in return —'

Špína heard no more and, himself invisible to the couple behind the bushes, he saw Frybort bend his head and kiss Márinka.

And she, whom he had worshipped from afar, did nothing. She neither screamed nor did she ward him off, nor did she call for help.

The happy lovers walked on, engrossed in each other. Špína stood rooted to the spot, staring into space and emptiness. Awaking from his trance-like stupor, he ambled away, head bent, a heavier frown on his face than would ordinarily have suited a philosopher.

Mrs Roller, the mayor's widow, more powerful and stricter than the mayor himself, did not relinquish her position with the mayor's demise. She censored all and sundry, her finger was in every pie and, above all, no one was safe from her sharp tongue. Having wandered through the woods, she caught sight of Mrs Roubínek and stopped to have a chat with her.

Lottie danced almost without a pause, but in spite of that she felt dissatisfied. She had had great plans for the evening and they had failed utterly. Vavřena, that energetic, handsome youth, had captured her affection which she mistook for love. She rather favoured him and felt flattered by his polite attention. Vavřena was known to be indifferent to girls, and it would have pleased her vanity if she could have boasted of this conquest. Oh, how she had hoped and wished for him to tell her of his love, to bare his soul to her in the course of the celebrations.

She felt miserable with disappointment. It is true, Vavřena had welcomed her upon arrival, but he had left her a little later, and had not returned at all as though she weren't there. Disgraceful!

He had even been late for the quadrille, in which he should have partnered her. Surely, surely that could be no accident, it must have been intentional. Lottie felt mortally offended.

Her affection for him vanished like a whiff of wind, hurt vanity took its place. She vowed she would ignore him and punish him for his offence.

In spite of everything, however, Lottie still waited for him to come to her, to beg for favours. So far, he had apologized and left; she had not seen him since. Perhaps she had hurt his feelings, perhaps he did not dare, perhaps —

Lottie left the hall, flushed with dancing, and went across to her mother. The Roller woman was saying goodbye to Mrs Roubínek.

'Come here, Lottie, *komm, komm, mein liebes Kind. Bedenke nur! Die Leny!*'

'What's happened?'

She was told what her mother had just learned from Mrs Roller. Lottie flushed with anger and, twisting her mouth proudly, she laughed contemptuously.

'Ah, here she is, here she is,' Mrs Roubínek exclaimed as she noticed Lenka, who was approaching them.

'My heartiest congratulations,' Lottie said bitingly.

'Well, well, still waters certainly do run deep,' her mother added, as she looked at Lenka spitefully. Lenka, however, stood there calmly, without a word to anyone, prepared for anything.

She had indeed expected spiteful remarks, unkind

74

laughter and a storm; she had endured so much in the past, the future held little enough fear for her. Within herself she felt triumphant, for she had gained a victory. Come what may, she was not lonely and deserted any more, her future held enough warmth and brightness to overcome this freezing disapproval.

Oh, the *Majales*!

The day was drawing to its close. The last rays of sunshine travelled over the woods, sweeping over mossy ground, upwards along the tree-trunks until they disappeared in the crowns high above the ground. The merrymaking was at its height, the band played almost continuously, hilarious laughter and jokes could be heard far and wide, the students' singing sounded with unabated force.

A group of them had settled down lower in the woods, some sat on rough benches, others under trees or on the grass, but one and all they lifted their pewters frequently to their mouths. They sang and laughed and joked. Špína alone did not take part in all the gaiety; he sat a little apart from them on the very edge of the bench, his head resting on his hand. His castor was pushed to the back of his head, the tails of his coat fluttered limply over the back of the bench, looking like broken wings.

'Špína,' one of his friends called, 'what on earth is the matter with you! Why the dejected attitude?'

'Mind your own business and leave me alone!' was the surly reply. Špína then looked deep into his pewter.

'Has anyone seen Zelenka?' the former asked again. And someone else replied:

'Of course nobody has seen him, because he isn't here. I bet he's at home and swots, the miserable ninny. He's a careful one! He doesn't want to be questioned —'

'The hawk, I can see the hawk!' another student shouted suddenly, pointing his pewter at the Roller woman who, knitting bag dangling from her wrist, was advancing upon them nosily.

Laughter sounded from all sides.

'*Vivat commissarius!*'

'*Vivat doctissima!*'

'*Vivat Xantippe!*'

The students drank the health of the 'learned commissary' for, year-in year-out, Mrs Roller went to watch the public examination in philosophy, where she sat next to the learned members of the board and the invited guests, a Latin book in her hand.

Naturally, the candidates were far from pleased to have her there, for it was a well-known fact that she kept nothing to herself and the varying degrees of success were a subject of discussion not long after the examinations. The Roller woman certainly did not keep the golden rule to wash the school's dirty linen within its walls.

She seemed to understand for whom the toasts were meant, for she stopped and her small beady eyes roamed over the faces of the noisy students.

'*Vivat Horatius Flaccus!*' someone called, and another, louder voice added:

'But the one that's upside down!'

Boisterous laughter was the answer and pewters clinked anew.

The shaft struck home. Mrs Roller turned and hurried off, with the name of the Roman poet ringing in her ears. The cause of her discomfiture was this:

Before the last examinations, Father Germanus gave her and all the other guests a book by a Latin author. On passing her the book — perhaps unintentionally, who knows — he held it upside down and so the good lady sat there all through the exams with Horace in front of her, but upside down.

The students got a lot of satisfaction out of the occurrence and now, reminded of it by her presence, they became hilarious again. Again, Špína was the only one who did not join in their happy mood: he sat, and drank and drank. The more he drank the further back his bristling castor slipped. The expression of anger slowly left his face, only to be replaced by sadness and melancholy.

His heart was melting; from time to time he would turn towards his neighbour, and then back again to drink and to rest his weary head upon his hands.

'I say, I've a feeling there's something on your mind,' his neighbour said to him under cover of the noise and singing.

'Well I — yes, there is,' Špína answered in a subdued voice.

'Well, spill it then.'

'Oh, but not here, I couldn't.'

'Then let's go somewhere else.'

Špína got up and walked unsteadily behind his friend; they stopped under a gnarled oak-tree. Their friends followed them with their eyes. 'Soaked', they said and winked.

'Come on, let's get it over with.'

'You see, it's like this — I —' Špína started haltingly. 'You won't poke fun at me, will you? I'm all alone, I haven't got a soul, not anywhere —' his voice broke and tears rolled down his cheeks. 'Nobody cares for me — I'm an orphan — and you see — and —' The lanky student began to sob in good earnest.

His friend said soothingly: 'Wouldn't it be better if you stopped crying and told me what it's all about?'

'Oh, it's easy for you to talk, but what have I got? I'm nothing but an orphan, alone in the world —'

77

His friend laughed shortly. 'What a lot of beating about the bush coming from such a big orphan as you are. Come on, get it off your chest, whatever it may be.'

'There, I knew it! I knew you'd make fun of me, just like all the others. Everybody only laughs at me — I'll — I'm —' sobs shook his whole frame violently. He slid down onto the mossy bolder and buried his head in his arms.

His friend stood over him for a while, trying to calm him, but when he saw that Špína did not trust him any longer he left him and went back to the merry group of students, who crowded around him wanting to know the whys and wherefores.

'I tell you I know as much as you do. I expect he drank out of desperation and had one too many. You know what he's like when he's fuddled, he cries and doesn't trust a soul.'

'The weeping willow!'

'As opposed to us! *Gaudeamus!*'

'*Gaudeamus!*' was the thundering reply from all sides as pewters clinked once more.

The sun set behind the trees; the crowds were slowly making their way homewards and footpaths leading towards the town were filled with families who wanted to get home before nightfall. The younger generation, however, and especially the students, lingered on beneath the high crowns of the trees, enjoying themselves to the utmost.

The band was still playing and gay students' songs filled the cool night air.

Miss Elis too would have gone home with the older generation, had it not been for Márinka, Frybort and Vavřena who were so insistent that she had to give in. She sat down, a little apart from the rest and waited, her

78

thoughts far away. She had not seen Lenka any more since their heart-to-heart talk.

Vavřena went up to Lottie and Mrs Roubínek again, but his efforts were in vain.

The cloud of unpleasantness would almost certainly have passed again had it not been for Mrs Roller and her intervention; but when Mrs Roubínek heard that their tutor, whose sacred duty it surely was to be their host, had spent his time with that stubborn creature, Lenka, almost unchaperoned, that he had given her so much of his attention, she could not forgive this breach of courtesy, for that was how it appeared to her. Her Lottie, the richest and most beautiful of all, to be thus pushed aside for a mere country-girl! Vavřena sank low indeed in Mrs Roubínek's eyes. She had given him credit for better taste and manners.

Lottie did dance with him once more after all, but she was aloof and gave curt replies to all his remarks.

After a while Vavřena stopped making conversation too. And again, that angered her. She had meant to punish him, to make him apologize and beg for favours. Instead of that he was distant with her as if she had affronted him.

At other times Mrs Roubínek walked home in the midst of large company. Vavřena, trying to do his duty offered to see them home, or rather to look after Fricek on the homeward journey. He thought he could come back again afterwards.

'You needn't bother, Lenka will look after Fricek,' Mrs Roubínek said briefly.

He bowed politely and let his eyes rest on Lenka's face. She seemed serene, her features were as pure and fresh as if they were part of nature, and her eyes shone with love for him. They were trusting and happy, but they were determined too.

Dusk descended upon the woods.

The band left the dance-hall and walked down to the restaurant, where the laughter and shouting were unabated. The students fell in line with many jokes, in preparation for their homeward march. Naturally their platoon was not as numerous as it had been in the morning, for a number of the students had left their ranks to offer a manly arm to the ladies on their way back to Litomyšl.

Špína was among the last to march; he walked unsteadily by his friend's side. Although the lanky orphan had cried his fill, the mood of tipsy unhappiness still persisted.

A crowd of faithful merry-makers walked along behind the noisy students' legion. Miss Elis was among them, led by Vavřena on one side and on the other side by Márinka, whom she had entrusted to Frybort's loving care.

The final notes of music sounded through the town late in the evening. The march was over, the crowds had dispersed. Just in time, for clouds gathered in the sky, promising a shower.

On reaching home at last, Miss Elis — having handed Márinka over to her mother — found Zelenka engrossed in his studies.

'Mr Zelenka, how could you! If you didn't have time you should have made it, like all the others did,' his well-contented landlady disturbed him.

'I really haven't got the time, Miss Elis, honestly I haven't,' the skinny youth replied. 'I have to make my way first.'

'Oh you, you dry stick-in-the-mud! I can just see what you'll be like. I expect you'll throw all your books away and never read another line as long as you're alive,' Frybort put in his bit while placing the violets in a glass of water.

Frybort and Vavřena sat in Miss Elis's room far into the night, discussing the eventful day.

All of them felt pleased, only the fussy Miss Elis cast a slight gloom over their discussion: what would happen at the college and what were the Roubíneks going to do? Neither of the students seemed very worried at the thought.

Špína slept like a log, untroubled by what he had witnessed in the woods, forgetting that he was an orphan.

Night fell.

Lenka, half undressed, sat behind a little table in her tiny room. A candle was throwing an uncertain light over the pages of her book. The house was still and quiet, everyone else was fast asleep. She sat there looking into space, dreaming with open eyes. Now and again her eyes focussed on the open page which read:

> *'Twas twilight and the first of May —*
> *May's evening — was the time of love.*
> *The sweet voice of the turtle-dove*
> *Woo'd where the fragrant pinegroves sway.*

She looked up again as a faint, whispering sound came from outside and, blowing out her candle first, she went to the window and opened it. The air felt cool and pleasant, and a fine drizzle fell from the dark sky, murmuring gently as it touched the trees.

And as all trees and flowers stretched their parched, dry limbs towards the reviving shower, so Lenka felt an easing of her sorrows. She leaned out and listened to the pleasant sounds, forgetting the position she held in her uncle's house and all that it entailed. A feeling of happiness enveloped her: she was blissfully, gloriously in love. Memories no more than a few hours old crowded upon her mind: again she stood under the old tree watching the

81

tiny birds, the birds who were the only witnesses of her recent happiness. Would her beloved also think of them?

At that time Márinka was fast asleep, unaware of the drumming of the rain against the window. Her dreams led her back into the woods, where she repaid her debt once more.

7

A new day dawned and life resumed its normal course. The bells had tolled, the students were assembled at college. Their boisterous good humour and elation had disappeared, to be replaced by sober sense.

The religious instructor did not put in an appearance and the students remembered the dean's strict words that he would stay absent until he received an adequate apology. They discussed the situation, but before they could decide what course to take, some of them were summoned to the dean, Frybort and Vavřena among them.

The town's prophecy, Miss Elis's forebodings were coming true. A rigorous enquiry into the recent rebellion and the Majales started. Such things cannot be kept quiet, especially in a little country-town, as was proved soon enough. Without exception the town's citizens were on the students' side and many a young lady felt apprehension stir on hearing that the students might even be expelled.

Frybort was losing his patience with the questioning which was dragging on and on. This was not due to fear on his part but to Miss Elis's ceaseless sighs and lamentations and to the frown which had settled on Márinka's usually clear countenance.

Vavřena was his usual confident self; for a time he tried to reassure Miss Elis, but stopped when he saw it was of no avail.

Zelenka gave lessons, studied diligently, ate bread and fruit stew for supper, in fact he led his normal life. His face, faded before its time, showed some inner satisfaction.

Špína pretended a complete disinterest in the after-effects of the celebrations. He sat over an open book, smoking, a heavy frown upon his face, and stared into space.

Miss Elis, believing that the questioning and punishment weighed heavily upon his mind, tried to console him.

Špína turned to her before she could say more than a few words and said in a rumbling voice:

'Oh God, how I wish it would be over. I'd be only too glad if they threw me out!'

Miss Elis was aghast. The very thought that one of her boarders might be expelled filled her with horror. Forty-seven students had lived under her roof, all of them had been among the best, they had taken up important posts — and now this! Why, the good name of her lodgings was at stake!

She felt more restless than the students themselves. True enough, the whole town had taken the students' part, but there were a few exceptions after all and Mrs Roller and Mr Roubínek with his whole family must necessarily be among them.

The morning following the celebrations saw Mrs Roubínek giving her husband, who was dressed in the 'Colonel', an account of the previous evening. She told him at great length and not at all objectively how rude their tutor had been to Lottie and how badly he had behaved.

The story provoked Mr Roubínek intensely, especially

when he was told how Lenka had walked about the woods, enjoying the tutor's company.

Mr Roubínek looked away from King Herod a number of times and, had it not been time for him to repair to his office, he would have started an official investigation into the matter. Mrs Roubínek, however, was undaunted. As soon as her husband came home at lunchtime, she started on the subject again, quoting Mrs Roller as a witness. Lenka was in the kitchen then, but she had a fair idea of what was going on. Her uncle had directed many an icy glance at her during the meal and she understood his meaning plainly.

She felt no fear, in fact she was prepared for almost anything, nevertheless the thought of Vavřena weighed heavily on her mind.

The young tutor came at the appointed hour and was received coolly by the lady of the house. Lottie pretended to see him not at all. He tried to get a glimpse of Lenka — in vain. Her aunt was sure to have made her work at something that made it impossible for her to come into the room. As Vavřena was about to enter Fricek's room where the lesson was being held, he met the Roller woman in the corridor.

Mrs Roubínek welcomed her guest in honeyed tones and kept her until Mr Roubínek came home from work.

The poor wretch — everything seemed to have slipped out of control.

Mrs Roller not only confirmed but embroidered everything he had been told by his wife. She also added that Lenka was friendly with that Miss Elis who felt so patriotic that she would like to turn everything upside down; to prove her point she said Miss Elis had been great friends with the late Mrs Rettig who was known all over Litomyšl for her patriotic attitude.

85

As soon as the Roller woman left, Mr Roubínek made for Lenka's little room, dressed as he was in his service coat.

His niece sat near the window, sewing, as she had been bidden by her aunt. She was surprised to see him, for she could not remember her uncle ever having come to visit her here. He stood in the middle of the room and fixed her with his eyes. He asked her about the previous day, Vavřena and Miss Elis, as if conducting an official enquiry.

Lenka's answers were straightforward and quite firm, with no thought of denial or concealment. The enquiry seemed to be over, when her uncle's glance fell on the table.

'What's that under the sewing?'

Lenka felt flustered.

'Hand it over.'

There was no way out for her.

Mr Roubínek picked up the slim volume and gave it a fleeting glance. Upon noticing that it was written in Czech, he asked her whose it was.

'It's mine,' Lenka lied, wishing to shield Vavřena.

'Oh! It's yours, is it? And since when have you been receiving presents, pray?' he said pointing to the inside cover, where his son's tutor had signed his name. She did not answer and a slow blush spread across her features.

It was too late to tell the truth now. Her uncle left the room without another word, the precious book imprisoned under his arm.

Later in the evening Mr Roubínek had a candle lit, which was not his custom, and sitting down in his coloured 'Colonel' he opened the *corpus delicti* and started to read.

Poor Mácha!

Unreasonable critics had scorned his poem, *May*, before, and now it was being judged — and scorned — again by Mr Roubínek.

If either Vavřena or Frybort could have seen that cold impassive face bent over those ardent verses, they would have roared with laughter.

His wife and daughter had gone to bed already, the house was still and quiet. Roubínek sat in his chair, holding the book in his bony hand, and read and read. It seemed to be a great effort, for he was unused to Czech books and, to make matters worse, this one was in rhymes, as he chose to call it.

He was unmoved by Mácha's glowing, poignant verses, his face remained unchanged; after a little, reading became an effort to him.

He put the book down for a while, but changed his mind and picked it up again to investigate it properly, as was his apparent duty. He read on, this time in whispers.

Again after a little while his lips stopped moving. His eyes, however, roved over the verses, he turned a page and whispered for a while, and then once more he was silent. He stared at one and the same spot, his eyelids drooped; the tassel on his nightcap bobbed, his tired head fell forward on his chest — he was asleep at last.

Unheeded lay the last verses of the third canto:

'Twas twilight — and the second of May
May's evening is the time of love.
To love's caresses the turtle-dove
Calls.

Woe, Roubínek, woe!

Mr Roubínek had apparently got up on the wrong side of the bed. He felt cross and bad-tempered, perhaps because of the nightmares he had had all night. Arrests, chains and a policeman far more terrifying than the good

87

Kmoníček, gallows, skeletons and suchlike were mixed up in his dreams from which he had awoken sweating and terror-stricken.

He felt sure his restless night was due to that 'book of rhymes'.

The thought that his ward read such heathen books, that she borrowed them from his son's tutor made his hair stand on end. But then, he had always thought him a patriot and an innovator. Mr Roubínek set out for his office fretfully.

Mrs Roubínek met Mrs Roller during the morning and the two ladies had a long talk. The latter said she had been to see the dean from whom she had found out many things. Before many hours had passed the town was buzzing with the story that Miss Elis's lodgers were worse off than the rest and that at least two of them would be expelled.

Mrs Roubínek told her husband all about it after lunch, when he had lit his pipe, thus relieving some of his ill humour.

Lottie sat in an easy-chair under the window and looked maliciously at Lenka, who was busy folding the table-cloth, and saw her stop and tremble, and look up at her aunt.

'Let me tell you, that young man will end badly one of these days. You mark my words and see if I'm right. To be so young and to consider innovations right and on top of that to start a riot! Well, really, what more is there to say? In my opinion he deserves the severest punishment,' Mr Roubínek said coldly, while exhaling a cloud of smoke.

Lenka, who had stood rooted to the spot, lifted her head and left the room. She felt indignant and exasperated at such unfeeling narrow-mindedness.

As soon as she had gone her cousin said: 'Won't she raise Cain!'

'I expect she'll turn even more stubborn than she is. *Na, es wird sich zeigen!*'

Márinka's mother visited Miss Elis during the day and caused her great anxiety by telling her what she had heard about the students, especially about Vavřena and Frybort.

Miss Elis sat in her room with a troubled mind, praying for her lodgers to come home soon.

At last, after what seemed ages, there was a heavy footstep on the stairs and Frybort breezed into the room.

'Oh Mr Frybort, how glad I'm you've come. I've been sitting here with my heart in my mouth. Now tell me quickly, is anything happening? Please tell me! Where have you been?'

'I? I've been questioned again, that's all.'

'Oh dear! And is it true that they'll ... that you'll be expelled?'

Frybort laughed. 'They'd have to expel all of us, you know. We're all for one and one for all.'

'But what if they do, what if they do expel you all!'

He laughed again.

'For shame! How can you laugh? The disgrace of it, why, it doesn't bear thinking about!'

'I've done nothing to be ashamed of. Do you call defending an old custom disgraceful?'

'No, no, of course not, but you won't be able to go on studying.'

'Look here, Miss Elis: I know enough to be a good citizen. And as for the rest, well, I'd never be much of a success as a bookworm, you know.'

'But what about Márinka?'

'What about her? She loves me and she'll marry me whether I'm a farmer in village or a successful lawyer in a big city.'

89

'All right. But what would Mr Vavřena do if they expelled him?'

'They won't do anything of the sort, I assure you. They'll think twice before expelling so good a student as they have in Vavřena. And anyway, Father Germanus is sure to stick up for him. After all: *ex moribus primam, cetera eminenter!*'

Miss Elis, having been landlady to so many generations of students, had caught enough Latin from them to understand Frybort.

'I pray to God you're right. Have they finished with the questioning?'

'Yes, it's over and done with. We ought to hear the verdict tomorrow.'

'And Mr Vavřena? Where is he?'

'Why Miss Elis! What a question! He's gone to give his lesson, of course.'

Vavřena walked upstairs and looked about, hoping to catch sight of Lenka, but the corridor was empty and the door to her room was shut. This was the second day he had not seen her and oh! how he longed for a glimpse of her. He knew this was no accident, he was sure Mrs Roubínek prevented her. Neither mother nor daughter took much notice of the young tutor as they had been wont to in the days prior to the celebration.

The peculiar thing was that Mr. Roubínek was at home. Vavřena gave his lesson. Lottie, whose habit it had been to fetch something from the room every so often, did not stir. When the lesson was over, Mr Roubínek, enthroned in his armchair and looking at King Herod, stopped Vavřena and spoke to him. He told him in his cold, indifferent manner that he was an official, whose duty it was to see that order and discipline were maintained.

Mr Vavřena obviously did not see eye to eye with him, for he took part in things which did not concern him. One day he would come to even greater harm than now. He should study and not take part in riots and patriotic actions, leading others astray as well.

'Žižka and the Emperor Joseph were the best two Czechs that ever lived,' but he did not add 'our church is a memorial of them,' instead he said 'and they didn't read such silly, heathen books with which you befuddle girls' brains. What do girls want with books? Ladles are much more suitable for them. Apart from that I'd like Fricek —'

'Sir, will you kindly come to the point?'

Mr Roubínek's eyes left King Herod and turned to the daring young man, a sure sign of his amazement and surprise.

'The point is ... I want another ... here's your money for the month, that's all.' He pointed to the table where Vavřena's salary for May had been put.

Vavřena remarked that he had not earned the money yet, thanked them and left without it.

Mrs Roubínek and her daughter were taken aback. They had expected Vavřena to be thunderstruck and to apologize humbly. And instead — he had bowed and left with proudly lifted head.

'Oh, the arrogance of him! The conceit! When I think of how we overestimated him!' Mrs Roubínek cried.

Vavřena did not go home from there. He sauntered through the town and towards the Nedošín woods. He was so deep in thought that he walked up to the old gnarled tree in the woods quite involuntarily. He looked up in surprise and there, above his head, was the bird's nest Lenka had been so thrilled with.

He walked on and on until finally he sat down on a

91

bench under an old birch-tree and let his thoughts stray
back to the happy moments he had spent with Lenka under
'their tree'.

What did the future hold for them? How was he to
get in touch with her?

It was long past supper-time when Vavřena came
home at last. He stopped in Miss Elis's room.

'Miss Elis, d'you remember what you said would
happen? You were right.'

'Oh dear, did they tell you not to come again?'
She looked up at him anxiously.

'Yes, that's exactly what happened. It may harm me
now, but it won't make any difference in the long run,
I expect. Still —'

'I understand, Mr Vavřena. We'll just have to look
at the bright side of things, that's all there is to it. And
anyway, loyalty is a virtue, whatever some people may
think,' she added significantly.

'Yes, I know and I quite agree with you. And I will
stay true and loyal, but you'll have to stand by me.'

Miss Elis gave him her hand, which he took gratefully.

8

The enquiries and negotiations in the college seemed endless. Many people expected things to turn out badly, the town was a-buzz with the worst rumours. The religious instructor, the dean and the episcopal commissary were agreed that the students had committed a grave offence and that punishment must be meted out severely.

The religious instructor was unshakable in his demands for 'adequate satisfaction' for the humiliation he had been forced to suffer. Luckily for the students the dean was not on the best of terms with him; he sided with them quite spontaneously and his task was made easier by the students themselves, who maintained throughout the questioning that they had not meant to demonstrate against the professors. It was the letter — they said — that had upset them to such an extent. The *Majales* had certainly not been a manifestation aimed against their teachers which they had proved by shouting '*vivat*' to the school and to the professors before the parade.

They were staunchly supported by Father Germanus, who defended them warmly in the dean's office.

In spite of that, however, the dean would hardly have reversed his decision if some of the leading citizens of the town had not pleaded on behalf of the students. This might have lessened the punishment of most of them, but the ringleaders, the 'brains' would not have escaped its most extreme form — expulsion from the school. And again, luck was on the students' side. The whole story was repeated in full detail to the dean's neighbour, who laughed at it uproariously and wished the students well.

He was a rich landowner who lived in the beautiful old Manor, and a word from him was like a seed sown in fertile soil. Count George was the *deus ex machina,* whose word sufficed to calm all troubled waters.

A deputation to the religious instructor, some *primae e moribus* and a few hours of incarceration were the final consequences of the riot and the unlawfully held students' May Day festival.

Next Sunday morning saw Frybort setting out for college with pretended sadness — punishment was to be served out that day. Miss Elis felt indignant and exasperated with her lodger for — imagine! — he thought the whole thing a huge joke.

Vavřena also left in high spirits, only Špína went grumbling like a bear.

Miss Elis did not leave her rooms that day. Forty-seven students had been her lodgers and none of them had ever given cause for trouble. Some of them even held high positions — and now! three students in disgrace, all at once.

She derived some satisfaction from the fact that there were others equally afflicted in the town, and that her students were, after all, among the best and cleverest, as they had proved. Not that she was glad that they had incurred punishment, but at the same time she could not, would not commend Zelenka's behaviour, nor did she address a word to him all day.

94

The town felt pleased with the outcome of the affair; only Mrs Roller remarked that she would have settled the matter differently if it had been up to her, and Mrs Roubínek, although a trifle disappointed, was satisfied to see the students punished.

Fricek had a new tutor before the week was out, a studious young lad whom the dean had recommended for his honesty and diligence, of which he had more than the college asked for.

Lottie and her mother welcomed him most kindly in the beginning, but they cooled off considerably within a few days. What was the use, thought Lottie who cared nothing for education, the new tutor was as well-informed as Vavřena, but as for his looks! The difference was enormous. On top of that he was shy and seemed to be afraid of them. He said good-day upon arrival and bowed politely and said the same before he left, and never two words between.

'I suppose he's all right, *aber unbeholfen*,' was Lottie's verdict, with which her mother agreed heartily.

Had Lenka wanted to be truthful she could have told them that the new tutor was anything but *unbeholfen*, in fact that he was the exact opposite. He was skilful and adroit. Within a week of taking up his post — lo and behold — she had a letter and a book which he had smuggled in very successfully.

The letter said:

'Brož is a good fellow. Trust him. I walk through the woods often, all's well with the old tree. I feel lonely there, though, but I hope and trust that I will find my lost companion again. How I long to talk to you! Will you send me a few lines too? I shall write more next time, for now just all the best! Sincerely yours, V.'

She read it, not once or twice, but whenever she was

95

alone during the day, and regularly every evening in her little room.

Brož carried her answer back a few days later. Vavřena hurried off to the Manor park where he looked for a shaded spot. He found one under a clump of trees, and sat down to open the letter which he read eagerly:

'You have made me very happy. Hope and faith are giving me strength. Give my love to the woods and to our tree.'

Hope and faith! The young man repeated the two words over and over again and fell into a blissful reverie.

Spring passed and summer came.

Frybort was gay and happy and, as the end of term was drawing near he began to study in good earnest. He saw Márinka frequently and, more often than not, he came home with a fragrant bunch of flowers. Although he was always in a good mood, he refused to tell where they were from. Miss Elis did not betray his secret and Márinka's mother never got an opportunity again to point out that his coat was dusty.

Špína alone could have given him away, but nothing was further from his mind. He was more taciturn than ever, surly and bad-tempered, and smoked and studied at such a rate that Miss Elis began to have her doubts. Vavřena, on the other hand, spoke to Miss Elis whenever they were alone, and always about Lenka whom Miss Elis herself would have liked to meet again. She had come to love her — the niece of her own beloved George, and she would have welcomed the opportunity for Lenka to come and live with her.

She knew Vavřena well enough to trust him and she was sure that the two young people would be happy together for the rest of their lives. Her mind was busy calculating how much longer Vavřena would have to study before achieving a secure enough position to be able to get married. She could not visualise him at the altar with anyone else but Lenka. —

Brož gave his lessons to Fricek conscientiously, which pleased the master of the house. Mr Roubínek told his friend, the notary, during one of their cosy talks that he liked the new instructor mostly because he was modest and not at all flighty, and took no notice of things that were no concern of his, as befitted a young man of his station. Lenka too was grateful to the youth, though for different reasons. The exchange of Czech books and letters was running smoothly with his help.

Although Vavřena was often in the vicinity of their abode, he caught a glimpse of Lenka very rarely; her aunt watched her like a hawk. But even an occasional glimpse of Lenka was enough to make him happy for a time. Soon, however, he wanted more than just to see her from afar, he wanted to talk to her, to hear her voice. And there, Miss Elis came to his assistance.

Lenka had been forbidden to attend the Students' Mass so that she had to go to services held at the Manor church. There, unbeknown to her aunt and uncle, she met Miss Elis who was more than happy to be able to exchange a few words with her.

One Sunday morning Miss Elis brought Márinka along and the two girls became friends. Naturally Márinka attended Students' Mass otherwise, but she had been happy to make so small a sacrifice. The secret shared by Vavřena, the nice Miss Elis and her beloved Frybort thus became her secret too.

Márinka invited Lenka for a walk in the Manor park for Sunday afternoon if she were free. There, she said, they could have a good, long talk.

And so, while Mr Roubínek fixed King Herod with an unblinking stare and conversed with his friend, the notary, at the same time, while Mrs Roubínek sat in the room with them and listened, while Lottie was out visiting her friends, Lenka left the house and hurried to the park where Márinka awaited her. The park was not very crowded at that time of the day, for the woods outside the town attracted people more. Be that as it may, two other people were attracted to the park just then: two students of philosophy, who suddenly appeared between the trees and joined the young ladies in their walk.

The happy moments in the park were all too short, but they were long enough for all that to convince Vavřena of Lenka's true and faithful love, of her pure heart and generous mind; to Lenka they meant even more: she gathered strength and courage from her memories for weeks on end. And while the two were engrossed in serious talk, Frybort entertained Márinka with his wit and sense of humour.

Both Vavřena and Lenka were sorry that they could not meet regularly every day, sometimes not even every Sunday. Several weeks passed occasionally before Lenka could tell Márinka that she would be free again.

And so the lovers had no other choice but to write each other letters, which their conscientious *postillon d'amour* delivered with precision.

There was a fair at the Nedošín woods on the Sunday following St Antony's day. Again the woods were crowded. Mrs Roubínek and Lottie passed a pleasant afternoon among the gentry.

Mrs Roller arrived a little later, but she was full of news for Mrs Roubínek. Since nothing was allowed to escape her attention for long, she knew all about Vavřena's and Lenka's meetings.

Mrs Roubínek stood aghast. How could her ward so forget herself! Oh, she would attend to her!

Lottie saw that all her hopes were ruined.

Lenka was alone at home. She sat at the window of her little room, looking out into the garden, while her thoughts wandered back to the park and to Vavřena. Suddenly there was a rustling outside her door and the next moment her aunt, still in her outdoor clothes, was in the room with her. An inquisition started. Lenka did not deny the accusations, nor did she tell any lies. She said, yes, she had been to the park and she had met Vavřena there and spoken to him.

Mrs Roubínek, expecting anything but these calm statements, was beside herself with rage. There was no bending the proudly lifted head! She called her husband to assist her and a real storm broke out. The outcome of it was that Lenka was strictly forbidden to go anywhere near the park or to speak to Vavřena. Should Lenka disobey her uncle and her aunt, all care and loving kindness would be withdrawn from her and she could pack her bags and join her no-good boy-friend.

The Bishop of Hradec himself came to Litomyšl in July to be present at the students' examinations. He was especially keen to probe their knowledge in religious matters.

The studies began to tell on Zelenka's health, for he got thinner day by day.

On the eve of the great day Špína asked Miss Elis for a big cup of black coffee because he intended to study all night long. Miss Elis stayed up with her students on such occasions. However, ten o'clock had hardly struck when Frybort shut his book with a bang and said: 'Whatever I know will have to do. I can't learn it all overnight, anyway.'

He went to bed and was fast asleep in no time. Vavřena shut his book at eleven, and soon after sleep overwhelmed him too. Špína drank his mug of coffee to overcome all sleepiness. The Scriptures lay open in front of him, he read and smoked. Greyish clouds wafted across the low room like fog high up in the mountains, making Zelenka's pale face barely visible. Zelenka himself sat slouched over his script and studied, or — as Frybort was apt to put it — swotted by the light of a little oil-lamp.

Miss Elis sat in her own room at the window, looking out into the cool, dark night. She hoped and prayed her students would not disgrace her. There was no doubt in her mind about Zelenka and Vavřena, Frybort had a better head than most, and Špína — well, Špína had been very diligent of late. What Miss Elis did not know, however, was that Špína only sat over his books while his mind was God knows where. At midnight Miss Elis left her chair and opened the door to the adjacent room. She heard the even breathing of the sleepers, she saw Zelenka sitting over his script, wide awake, and over there in the corner sat Špína with the open book in front of him. His cup was empty, the coffee gone — could that be snoring? Miss Elis did not trust her ears. Surely he could not drink the coffee and — fall asleep!

'It's too much for him,' Miss Elis thought, 'one cannot study all the time. Perhaps I ought to wake him up, oh dear, I really don't know what to do, it's so late and I'm sure he's tired out.'

In the end she left him where he was and went to bed herself.

She wished the students all the best in the morning and reminded them to cross themselves with holy water. She was on tenterhooks while they were gone and spent half her time looking out of the window. Márinka was in

100

and out of the kitchen the whole time, as badly worried as Miss Elis. Their conversation centred only around the students and what they were doing at that very moment.

The bells announced mid-day, the warm air trembled with their sound, another half-hour passed when at last the longed-for voices sounded in the hall below. Miss Elis dropped her spoon and hastened into the corridor.

She could hear Márinka's voice from below, as well as Frybort's laughing answer. The result must be good indeed! Then Zelenka appeared, his pale face flushed, a smile upon his lips.

'*Omnia eminenter,* Miss Elis!'

'Congratulations and welcome, Mr Zelenka. You certainly deserved it.'

Vavřena was right behind him, a little calmer, but happy too. The last of them was Frybort, who called to her from the stairs:

'Oh, Miss Elis, I'm not as good as Zelenka, but I didn't get the bird!'

'I'm relieved to hear it, that would have been no feather in your cap!'

'Well, we can't all be among the best, can we. My course is fair to middling.'

'And thank the Lord for that. Where's Mr Špína, didn't he come back with you?'

Vavřena and Frybort were silent for a moment, then Vavřena replied: 'I'm afraid he's out of luck, as usual.'

'What a pity. He tried so hard, whatever will he do?'

Miss Elis's day was spoilt for her. She had felt quite sure that Špína would pass adequately at least.

They waited for him for a long time; in vain.

'Maybe he didn't want to spoil the day for us,' Vavřena said, 'I can tell you I certainly don't feel as happy as I might have done if Špína had been here with us.'

101

Špína himself spent the hot, quiet afternoon in the Manor park where he had taken refuge in a shaded spot under a gnarled fir-tree. His chin was resting on his hand, his eyes cast down to the ground.

He was slowly coming out of the stupor which had mercifully clouded his thoughts when he received that stunning blow. He was trying to decide what course lay open to him, and sat there for a long, long time, motionless. At last he got up and left the park with measured steps which quickened as he got nearer to the centre of the town, for he thought that people turned their head to look at him and to make remarks and snigger.

Miss Elis was alone when he got home at last. She brought him his food and everything she could think of to make things easier for him, and never said a word which could have hurt his feelings.

Špína ate little enough. Turning his head to her, he said: 'I expect you've heard —'

'Yes, I've heard, and I'm surprised, to say the least of it, because I know how hard you worked.'

'There's nothing I can do about it.'

'Isn't it a waste of time! Won't you lose a year?'

'No, I shan't because I won't repeat the class. I seem to have been born under an unlucky star.'

'Well then, what do you intend to do instead?'

'I'll tell you since you ask me. I'll become a monk.' His voice sounded hollow as he said this.

'Oh, I shouldn't if I were you. And anyway, you can't, you failed in Scriptures!'

'Then I'll enter a monastery which will be willing to accept me in spite of that.'

'Oh God, have mercy on us, you can't mean that, Mr Špína!'

However, his mind was made up. He explained how

102

difficult things were for him financially, how hard he had to work for every crust of bread. 'I'd only hound myself to death if I stayed here, and nothing would come of it in the end, I'm sure. There are other reasons, too, why I can't stay on here, you know.'

Miss Elis, standing a little to the side, said compassionately: 'I know. You see, I —'

The student made a violent movement with his head.

'You know? Where — what — but that means that everybody will make fun of me.'

'Why, Mr Špína, what do you take me for?'

Not another word escaped him. He managed to keep his face non-committal and to give a general appearance of calmness in spite of the fact that his feelings were in a turmoil. He got up from his chair a little later and went slowly to his room. Miss Elis, looking at his bent, shabbily dressed figure, felt her throat constricting.

Once inside his room, Špína went over to the window and looked out. The square below was uncommonly lively. There were crowds of students, promenading up and down, gesticulating, in high spirits. Carts went by, filled up to overflowing with students' bags and cases, and proud fathers walked beside their offspring. There were many townspeople and villagers, a number of whom were dressed in national costume. All of them had come to fetch their sons, to take them home for their vacations. Špína sighed. There was no cart waiting for him, he had no father, no kind and loving mother who would expect and welcome him.

His eyes rested on the opposite side of the square; a farm-waggon drawn by a sturdy brown horse stood there, loaded with a trunk and a bundle of bedding wrapped up in striped sheets. A small secondary-school student stood by the horse's head; most probably he had lain awake all night, unable to sleep with excitement and longing. He stroked the horse's head, whispering to him that he had missed him and that he was happy to be going home to mother. The boy seemed to be bursting with impatience while his father settled the landlord's bill.

Špína felt shaken by the simple little scene he had witnessed. As if in answer, his mind produced pictures of his own boyhood: the old white mare, belonging to his uncle, which came to fetch him, year in year out, to take him to his parents, who lived in the same village. He remembered how he had always welcomed it and stroked it, how, after a long journey, he had looked out for his mother, who would always come a little way to meet him. Oh, and how his uncle had always praised him when he brought home good marks.

All these simple pictures of his happy youth flashed through his mind and as the dreamlike visions vanished, Špína leaned against the wall and bitter tears rolled down his cheeks.

Litomyšl was a happy town indeed that day, but there were a few exceptions. Many a young lady felt sad and lost at the thought that the students would be gone for a few months, and that some of them would not return at all but would continue their studies at the university in Prague, that noisy town pulsing with life, where they might so easily forget them.

Lenka's eyes too were full of tears although she tried hard to force a smile upon her lips.

She was forbidden to talk to Vavřena under threat of severe punishment, but what did she care for threats, why should she worry about punishment!

She went to the forbidden spot in the park at dusk. She did so secretly, defying her aunt's authority, knowing that what she did was wrong, for it was almost dark and she was unchaperoned. If she did not go, however, Vavřena would leave without a word from her, and she had to see him come what may.

The golden glow of the setting sun had faded, the woods were dressed in darkness. Lenka wanted to go home. They walked on a few steps, then they stood still again. Time passed, careless of their feelings. Lenka gave Vavřena her hand and he held it in his own when, all of a sudden, he took her in his arms and pressed his mouth upon her soft lips. She stood there, motionless in his embrace, and through the dusky shadows of the evening he saw the paleness of her face and the trembling of her silky lashes. Suddenly she freed herself and walked away with hurried steps. Her light dress appeared now here, now there among the foliage, a gate creaked in its hinges, and Lenka was gone.

'Remember' seemed to tremble in the air, as fervently as she had said it, Vavřena still felt her passionate kiss on his lips. He stood there watching the path, long after she had gone. Night fell.

Prent's Inn was brightly lit and gay with noise and laughter. The students, who were to leave for their vacations in the morning, had decided to meet there and celebrate the end of term. They were a merry lot, and singing, witty jokes and laughter followed each other in quick succession. They laughed uproariously when Frybort told them of the misfortune which had befallen Mrs Roller in church that morning. The story had spread like lightning through the whole town straight away, so that most of the students had heard it once before at least, nevertheless they doubled up with laughter when Frybort told it in his funny way.

During High Mass, Mrs Roller had pushed her way up

105

to the choir and sat down right by the banister, the inevitable knitting bag in front of her. While her mean little eyes flitted about here, there and everywhere, somebody standing close-by noticed that her knitting-bag was open and a strange object was lying right on top. When she turned back again and her glance fell on her bag, an involuntary cry escaped her. She pulled herself together and tried to retrieve the bag which was slipping over the banister as if of its own volition. She bent forward and noticed that people craned their necks and stared at her in wonder and surprise, for playing-cards fluttered out of her bag and settled down like giant snowflakes.

The town rocked with laughter at Mrs Roller's pack of cards, but no one got as much fun out of the episode as the students in Prent's Inn. It was getting late, but the laughter and the noise were unabated.

The mild July night lay lightly over the town. A few people stayed in front of their houses until midnight and then they went inside. The strumming of a guitar came from an open window somewhere, and when that stopped there was utter silence everywhere.

In an alcove of the ancient house in which she lived, Márinka sat by the open widnow. Sleep eluded her. She had a lovely view from where she sat: she saw the town square and the streets leading into it, and the town hall a little further down; the dark, star-lit sky stretched endlessly above her head. Miss Elis had told her that Frybort had left earlier in the evening. Was he back by now, she wondered? Oh, the long, long time ahead with Frybort gone, how could she make it pass fast enough?

All of a sudden the dark street below came to life with deep, muffled voices and Márinka, startled, left her seat hurriedly, while listening intently at the same time. There — there was the voice she knew so well, she recognized

106

it quite distinctly. Goodness, a serenade! For her, of all people! The song was lovely in itself and became even more so as it trembled in the still night air. She went to the window again, but she was careful this time. The sight which met her eyes thrilled her beyond words: she saw the singers, Frybort, whom she recognized at once, and friends of his. She noticed that windows were being opened across the way and people stood there looking out and listening; Márinka fled from the window again. What an honour!

The song came to an end, the footsteps of the singers faded away into the night; a key was pushed into the front-door, then there were footsteps walking up the stairs and then — and then — yes, here they stopped right by her door. She trembled slightly, hesitated, and came a little closer.

'Márinka,' she heard a whisper, 'Márinka, good night my sweet, and happy dreams!'

How gladly she would have answered him and thanked him for the happy moments he had given her. But she dare not, must not answer him aloud, so she whispered only to herself: 'Good night.'

The door creaked and Frybort was gone. Silence and tranquillity reigned everywhere again, except in Márinka's heart. Good night!

The students' leave-taking was general. All roads leading from Litomyšl were filled with carts laden with their belongings, on their way home to the furthest corners of Bohemia and Moravia. Zelenka had left in the morning, Vavřena not much later, and now it was Frybort's turn. His father, who was a farmer, was an honest, well-kept man, thanked Miss Elis most sincerely for looking after his son so well and, in gratitude and with his wife's compliments, he presented her with all sorts of eatables. The gay

107

student took his leave quite happily, but when it was his turn to say good-bye to Márinka, who looked unhappy and dejected when he held her little hand in his, his serenity left him.

'The time will pass faster than you think. I'll be back before you know it, believe me. Good-bye for now!' he called cordially.

The town seemed dead without the students, for they were a happy, high-spirited crowd, the very houses seemed lost and lonely without their pranks and jokes and voices.

'Doesn't it seem as though we'd had a funeral here,' Miss Elis remarked to Márinka's mother.

'That's what it reminds me of too. It wouldn't be the same without them, would it, Márinka?' she said, turning to her blushing daughter.

'I feel as if my own sons had left me,' Miss Elis continued. 'Believe me, I like these boys better than any of the forty-seven students I had here before them.' But her thoughts centred on Vavřena and Frybort all the time.

'What about Mr Špína?' Márinka's mother asked.

'I feel so sad whenever I think of him — he's going to enter the monastery tomorrow.'

Špína meanwhile loitered about the whole afternoon. Towards evening people saw him in the Manor park where he sat under a tree, immersed in thought. On leaving the park he went straight home and begged Miss Elis not to let him oversleep, as he had to leave early in the morning.

'Do you mean to tell me you aren't going to say good-bye to anyone?'

'Well — eh — who to?'

'Márinka's mother, for instance.'

'Oh, I'll see her at the shop, I expect. I certainly don't intend to go to her rooms.'

Miss Elis was full of understanding.

'So you won't see Márinka any more,' she added gently.

'No, oh no, of course not. And I don't want to either.' His voice was hoarse. 'But will you — I mean, would you please tell her' — he turned a deep red — 'that I wish her well and I hope she'll always be happy.' That was all he said.

He slept little that night, the last night of his sad and troubled life here which, in spite of everything had been independent and free to a great extent. Oh, if he could only look into the future to know what was in store for him, he thought. There was little enough pleasure and happiness, whatever else there was, that he felt sure of.

Miss Elis put some food into his modest bundle in the morning. He had not expected to find leave-taking so sad and difficult. His voice shook while thanking Miss Elis for all she had done for him as he realized how good and kind she had been.

Miss Elis cried quite unashamedly and begged him to write whenever he found the time. He left the room and as he came into the corridor he stopped, unable to believe his eyes. It was very early in the morning and yet, there stood Márinka fully dressed, looking as pink and fresh as a rosebud. She stood near the staircase as if waiting for him. He walked up to her and opened his mouth, but speech would not come. His mouth was dry, his throat contracted and he felt paralysed, but his eyes were alive and spoke for him. Then he heard her pleasant voice, the voice which had made his heart beat faster so many times.

'You would have left without saying good-bye to me, Mr Špína! I couldn't let you go like that. Farewell and God bless you. Don't forget us altogether.'

It seemed to him that the dark corridor was suddenly full of light and air. A happy smile spread across his face,

109

and he felt confused and mumbled something, but his 'All the best' and 'God bless you too' were clearly audible.

The surprise meeting, causing him such joy and sorrow at the same time, was Miss Elis's doing.

Litomyšl was well behind him when he began to think coherently again. His bundle in his left, his cane in his right, he walked with a firm step towards the town of Vysoké Mýto; and as he reached the low hill he stood under an old poplar and looked back over the countryside and watched, for the last time, the town which he had grown so fond of and where he had spent the last few years. The air was bright and clear on this lovely August day. He saw the valley and the meadows and the woods, and they looked green and fresh to him. The houses presented a garden city amidst verdant splendour. Over there was the lovely Manor park, further on the college, so coldly heartless and yet so dear, a little further still the town hall, and right opposite it an ancient house with an alcove and there —

His gaze lingered on all these places, while he said good-bye to them for the last time. Farewell, my past, farewell youth and freedom, too!

Oh, for the years of student life!

They are years of joys and sorrow, years of intensive study and awe-inspiring examinations, years of gaiety and jokes and songs, years of wearisome tutoring and teaching, of a happy mind and healthy strength, of hardships and poverty and — in spite of that — years of glowing dreams, full of bright hopes and plans, of freedom and of friendship, of one's first lines of poetry and, above all, of first love. Is there anyone among you who wanted to part with his youth and freedom, and then remembering with his heart and soul, forever remembering, while life becomes glum and dreary?

110

9

Miss Elis was a veritable benefactress of young lovers; her flat became a branch post office. The postman had a letter for her whenever the coach arrived, but she rarely opened it.

She looked at the envelope and, seeing that it was marked, she put the letter away in her chest of drawers next to her prayer-books. Márinka would run in upon the postman's departure and ask eagerly:

'Is there anything for me?'

Her face lit up whenever Miss Elis smiled and said: 'Here's one from Moravia.'

Two letters chanced to come at the same time occasionally, and then Miss Elis would say:

'This one is for you, but the other one must be taken to the chapel in the park.'

Márinka still met Lenka there every Sunday, and whenever there was a letter for her she gave it to her there.

'Anything of interest?' Miss Elis would ask as soon as Márinka had glanced fleetingly at her letter.

'Only his best regards and sincere thanks, and he says he's looking forward to being back again.'

'I can well believe that. I expect you're looking forward too, aren't you?'

Frybort wrote to Miss Elis personally once or twice, Vavřena wrote more often. Zelenka did not write at all, and no sign of life came from Špína.

'The poor fellow has nothing to write about, except upleasant things,' Miss Elis said once while discussing him with Márinka.

The bright sunny days of the summer vacations passed all too quickly for the students and dragged on interminably for the young ladies left behind in Litomyšl.

Lenka was worse off now, since the *Majales*, than she had ever been before. Lottie seemed to have forgotten that they were cousins, her aunt was even stricter than before, and her uncle was of no help whatsoever, for his wife's word was law at home. Lenka could never do right no matter what she did, no matter how hard she worked or how well she looked after the household. Things reached such a point that even the staid citizens were beginning to notice the state of affairs and were remarking on it. They disapproved heartily and did not omit to say so. In their eyes Lenka was being turned into a Cinderella who was never given a chance to go anywhere or to do anything but household work.

They were wrong in spite of all appearances, for Lenka felt better when she was left to herself. Then she had time and opportunity to read her Czech books or to pore over Vavřena's letter to her heart's content, or just to sit and dream of what the future held in store for her.

Her aunt relaxed her reins and allowed Lenka to move about more freely as soon as summer vacations started. On Sunday mornings she attended services in the Manor church and spent the afternoons either in the park or at the cemetery, where her parents were buried. Márinka was her one and only friend, who brought her not only letters from Vavřena, but frequent invitations to Miss Elis's. Finally, on the third Sunday after vacations had begun, the two met at the cemetery, from where Lenka accompanied Miss Elis to her flat, as she had been longing to for a long time.

The afternoon looked doubly beautiful in the light, airy room, which was so neat and tidy.

Lenka stood there, in the centre of the room, her eyes fixed on her uncle's portrait. The bond between her and Miss Elis grew firmer as they stood next to each other, both moved by the face so dear to them.

Miss Elis also took Lenka to the students' room, and showed her where Vavřena had his table, where he used to sit and which was his favourite place. The room seemed empty and silent without him.

The weeks passed, letters came and went; Lenka visited Miss Elis and Márinka often during that time. When her aunt found out at last and forbade further visits, it was far too late, for autumn had already come.

While the fruit-trees ripened and grass and flowers faded, and as the birds made ready to fly to warmer parts, guests expected with such longing streamed back into Litomyšl from all sides.

Carts bulging with students' boxes and cases came from the farthest corners of the kingdom, the town seethed with life once more — the students were back.

Secondary schoolboys came together with the college students.

Life in Litomyšl returned to normal. Miss Elis's and Márinka's pleasure was great when Frybort returned and Vavřena followed his example. Zelenka also lodged with his former landlady again and fell into his old habits easily, studying, giving lessons, and living mostly on dry bread

113

and fruit stew. Only Špína was gone with never a word to say how life was treating him.

Brož took up his lessons with Fricek Roubínek again, acting anew as *postillon d'amour*, for Mrs Roubínek watched over her niece with even greater care since the students had returned. The lovers had no other choice but that of quill and paper.

Frybort was even happier than before; he lived in the same house as Márinka, he saw her every day without interference from her mother, who had guessed her daughter's secret anyway and had no objections.

So autumn came and went, the ground grew hard and the first snowflakes fell softly to the ground. Frybort was almost as busy and worried again as he had been in spring before the *Majales*.

As Christmas drew near people started to discuss and to look forward to the students' ball, which was one of the major events of the town. This year too, the committee — led by Frybort and a few others — was more than busy trying to make this ball the most beautiful and enchanting one that had ever been, as though aware that it would be the last one in the history of the school.

Lottie started with her preparations in good time. 'You mark my words, my precious, you'll be queen, *keine andere!*' her mother would remark while the sewing was under way. Lenka had the largest share in the preparations.

She did a lot of the sewing without a ray of hope that she would be permitted to attend the ball, while Lottie could hardly restrain her impatience. She had given up all hope that her aunt would take her too. This left her unmoved — unmoved but by no means indifferent. Oh, to be with Vavřena for a few blissful hours, to see him and to be able to talk to him! Wonders, however, never cease. A week before the ball was due her aunt remarked that if she wished to come with them she would have to start making preparations. No influence on her husband's part had brought about this miracle; people's gossip about her meanness and unkindness had achieved it.

The material of Lenka's dress was naturally inferior to Lottie's, but she was clever with her needle and made the most of it. Although she had little or no jewelry at all, her youth and her complexion made up amply for the lack.

The long-expected evening arrived at last. It was bitterly cold outside, the stars sparkled brightly in the sky. Mr Roubínek, bathed and shaved, paced up and down impatiently, waiting for his womenfolk.

He wore the 'Tattler', a black suit fitting him better than the other ones he had, which had inherited the name from its maker. Suddenly, the clear tinkling of bells was audible from outside as the sledge stopped in front of the house. Mr Roubínek knocked on the door leading to the ladies' dressing-room.

'Make haste, the sledge is waiting.'

'*Aber* Roubínek, the shots haven't been fired yet.'

Just then a terrific bang went off, and another followed straight away. The ball had begun. Lottie who was fully dressed stood in front of the mirror, looking at herself with minute attention. Her mother watched her with indulgence and approval, delighting in her youth and freshness, so well accentuated by the richly trimmed, tasteful dress.

'*Nein*, you will be queen of the ball, Lottie! *Wenn eine Dame schön sein soll, muss sie schön gewachsen sein*, and you certainly are, my love!' She looked at her again. '*Wenn eine Dame schön sein soll, muss sie dunkle Augen haben*, and you have those too! There, fix that bow, that's right. *Wenn eine Dame — schön sein soll — muss sie dunkles Haar haben*, and my precious has that too. *Aber* Roubínek!' she called peevishly when her impatient husband knocked

115

on the door again. '*Wie ich sag*, you shall be queen of the ball.'

The bangs were noisy in the frosty air.

'Do take care not to get your dress crushed. Ready Lenka?' she turned to her niece suddenly.

'Yes, quite ready.'

Lenka stood a little apart, neither humiliation nor envy spoiling the serene expression of her face. Within herself, however, she felt rather apprehensive at the thought of Vavřena; wouldn't he be sure to prefer her cousin in her gorgeous dress? She was her own severest critic, never dreaming that she looked like a rosebud on its graceful stem.

The door opened at last and Mr Roubínek batted his eyelids rapidly in astonishment: that ravishing creature, turned out like a queen, was his daughter! The family settled down in the waiting sledge after all the neighbours had dutifully expressed their admiration. They went off towards the Karlov which was ablaze with lights. The bridge leading to the inn was lined with chimney-sweeps, all of whom held burning torches in their hands. A little further on stood Kmoníček in dress uniform. A dense crowd of onlookers had gathered at the bridge; they had come to watch out of sheer curiosity and now they stood around and made remarks about the passers-by, of whom there seemed no end. The torches flickered in the wind, the mortars banged, and people kept coming all the time. They all made for the entrance to the inn and from there straight into the dance-hall, where the orchestra was playing a merry tune.

It was really pleasant in the hall, which was full of light and music. The students looked after the ladies well, and helped them pass the time agreeably. Lenka's heart thumped with apprehension and excitement as she

116

reached the hall, and a shiver went up and down her spine when the orchestra began to play.

She had never before, in all her life, attended such a grand social event.

Lottie was quite self-assured as she entered the big hall, and accepted the students' courteous bows with a gracious nod. Her eyes swept the hall with speed, giving everyone but a fleeting glance. There was one exception though: that was when she noticed the slim young man who stood at the side entrance.

She saw that Vavřena stood there, glancing at her as if in passing, coolly, that he turned his head away, and then — then — a startled movement, his face lit up, his apparent calmness deserted him.

Oh, the blind fool! She had expected more than the cool indifferent glance he had bestowed on her. His eyes had certainly shown joy, but not at the sight of her!

His gaze was fixed on Lenka in happy surprise. He had not expected her, never dreaming she would come. When Lenka noticed his startled movement, when she saw the joyful look on his face, she felt serene once more. But when he stood in front of her and asked her for the next dance, when he held her in his arms and whirled her around the hall while the orchestra played a gay and lively tune, and when, at last, she heard his ardent, loving words whispered into her ear while they danced, she thought her heart must surely burst with happiness.

Sofas and arm-chairs stood under the many heavy mirrors along the wall; the highest tribunal was seated there: the chaperons. Mrs Roubínek lifted her horn-rimmed *pinces-nez* elegantly and watched her daughter, who danced almost incessantly.

Lottie was surrounded by admirers during the interval while most other couples walked up and down the hall.

And yet, she felt far from satisfied: for there was only one person whom she had hoped to see that evening and he seemed to be unaware of her presence.

She waited in vain for him to come and talk to her. He danced with her cousin and, judging from his manner, seemed to enjoy himself. This was too much for the proud young lady, she turned away in a furious temper. Her mother's eyes, too, followed the happy couple everywhere with an unkind look.

Lenka and Vavřena, however, cared nothing for the harsh looks sent in their direction. They made the most of the few happy moments they had been granted, like Frybort, who gave all his attention to the elated Márinka.

'I wish Miss Elis could see us now!' Lenka whispered. 'She'd give us her blessing, I'm sure.'

At eleven o'clock or thereabouts a fanfare sounded from the gallery, where the orchestra had been placed. Count George, accompanying his lovely sister, had arrived at the ball. The last sounds of the fanfare died away and the music and the dancing were in full swing again.

Midnight came and went and Vavřena had still not come to pay his compliments to Lottie, a sure sign that he did not intend to come at all. She had lost her fight after all. She went up to her mother, a heavy frown upon her forehead.

'*Bedenke nur, wie er ungalant ist,*' she complained, but ample reward was in store for her: Count George, on his tour of the hall, stopped and spoke a few kind words to them. Mrs Roubínek was beside herself with joy and, passing Vavřena and Lenka on her way to her husband who was next door, she paused to look at them disdainfully. After all, how could they equal her? The student who was of peasant stock and that niece of hers — well, they were birds of a feather. Mrs Roubínek did not omit to inform all her friends of the pleasantries the Count had exchanged with her, and it took little more than a minute for word to get round that Lottie was to be the Queen of the Ball.

Mr Roubínek was worse off than anyone else. He did not drink, card games did not attract him, and there was no wall adorned with a picture of King Herod on which to turn his eyes. He was used to going to bed at an early hour — and here he was, stuck for the whole night! He yawned and longed for the 'Colonel', for his nightcap and, first and foremost, for his soft warm bed. He did feel pleased, however, that an aristocrat had deigned to speak to his wife.

The ball came to an end as the new day dawned. Frybort saw Márinka and her mother home, Vavřena accompanied them. Mr Roubínek and his family walked home too. Snowflakes danced in the half-light of the dawn and lay lightly on the ladies' coats and shawls. In spite of their tiredness the company talked mainly about the compliments paid by Count George. Lenka alone was quiet; no one would have guessed how happy she was or how hopeful of her future.

Her thoughts went back to Vavřena's words, to the solemn promise he had made in the solitude of the ball-room alcove:

'Keep faith, my darling, and remember I'll never fail you.' Lenka believed him with all her heart and soul.

10

Another spring came, bringing not only fresh flowers and new songs, but also the dawn of new times. All nations suffering under absolutism felt their prayers had been answered. Metternich was overthrown, censorship abolished, and permission was granted for the National Defence to be created. The new constitution was announced on March 15th and Prague and the whole Kingdom far and wide were in a turmoil of triumph and exultation. The National Defence Corps, or Guards, sprang into being almost overnight.

Above and beyond all others, college and university students influenced the happenings of the fast moving days. A students' legion, organized on the same lines as in ancient Rome, was created in Vienna and there were many more before long.

The peaceful town of Litomyšl changed overnight: everything was topsy-turvy, changes and upheavals followed each other in quick succession, news from Prague kept coming steadily, each item more exciting than the last. While some people welcomed the new constitution with open arms, others wavered, and the rest grumbled on the sly, for they would not hear of novelties and changes.

Mr Roubínek felt extremely unhappy. He was nervous and restless for, more conservative than most men, he felt nothing but apprehension, and foresaw the end of the old order and complete ruin of civilization.

Although his friend, the notary, visited him with an even greater frequency, the times of their cosy talks were a thing of the past. It is true, Mr Roubínek sat in his chair and fixed his eyes on King Herod as usual, but his gaze would falter and wander towards the notary, who was bursting with news.

There were riots in Vienna, Metternich was overthrown, Prague was full of confusion, public meetings were being held, censorship was abolished and serfdom too — dear me, where would all this lead to! Why, the new constitution was nothing but a monstrous upheaval of the good old order!

Guards units were created all over the countryside, Litomyšl would have one in no time, too. Every citizen would have to take up arms, wear a forage cap, go on parades, stand on guard and take part in manoeuvres!

It was enough to make anyone feel ill. Mr Roubínek could not take things easy any more; he did not even enjoy his pipe, although his Lottie had prepared it for him with her own loving hands.

There was too much noise and singing in the streets, as well as shouts like 'the nation, the country, freedom, equality, the mother tongue, local government' and suchlike. And, as Mr Roubínek remarked to his friend, God alone knew what other slogans the fatheads would invent.

Goodness knows where so much patriotic fervour had sprung from all of a sudden, almost overnight. Everyone seemed to be turning patriotic, respect and reverence were a thing of the past. Heads were held higher as though the

121

constitution had added inches to people's height. Mrs Roubínek felt ill at ease, for she heard little German spoken nowadays and her own Czech raised a quick smile now and then. Her husband and the notary were in complete agreement, and she found an equally good friend in Mrs Roller, with whom she could grouse and grumble to her heart's content.

'*Bedenken Sie*, how our Lenka has changed. You know what she was like: never a word to say for herself, as stubborn as you make them, and now — well, you'd be surprised. She's talkative and gay, and that's all because of —'

'*Diese Konstitution!* You mark my words, *man wird noch rauben und morden!*'

When Lottie came home and told them that the students had had a big meeting and had decided to create a students' legion, Mrs Roubínek sighed:

'That's the end! Giving the students swords instead of pens is the same as putting a razor into a child's hand, in my opinion. Believe me, that's the end!'

'*Und was die Professoren und was der Pater Rector?* Can't they do anything to stop it?'

'They can't, that's just it. What can they do when even the ministry has lost all respect!' Mr Roubínek gave King Herod an unblinking stare as he said this.

Miss Elis hardly saw her students all day long, except for Zelenka. They were either at college or attending endless meetings which, needless to say, neither Frybort nor Vavřena would have wanted to miss. All faculties and academies had created their students' legions, surely Litomyšl could not be among the last! There was no one to stop them and nothing to hold them back; and so, before long — even before the town had its own National Defence Corps — the students' legion went on parade, led by a captain and elected officers.

122

Márinka's mother often discussed the situation with Miss Elis, telling her more than once that she did not like such stormy times, which might do more harm than good. Miss Elis, however, being the kindly, enlightened soul she was, patiently explained the new constitution and all it stood for, for Vavřena had taught her to understand it well. She felt pleased with the turn of events, and happy that the patriotic spirit which had been so conspicuous by its absence in the town, had made itself felt at last.

'I wish Mrs Rettig could have lived to see what's happening now. What a pity she's gone!' and her eyes strayed to the portrait of Father George, who had been an ardent patriot during his lifetime.

Her flat became famous through her lodgers. She flushed with pleasure when Márinka came to tell her that Frybort and Vavřena had been elected officers at a big students' meeting.

'Oh dear, they'll have to have officers' sashes,' Miss Elis said thoughtfully.

'I'll make Frybort's, shall I?'

'Yes, and I'll make Vavřena's, because Lenka won't be able to, poor dear.'

Frybort happened to meet Márinka on the stairs while on his way home in the late afternoon.

'Good afternoon, officer!' said the happy girl roguishly.

'And a very good afternoon to you too, sweetheart. I'm not afraid of losing you any more, you know. Girls like coloured flashes, don't they?' He caught hold of her hand and gave her a quick kiss.

'That was an officer's kiss, in case you didn't know!'

The legion had their first drill on the following day, which was Sunday. A small celebration was held in Miss Elis's flat in the early afternoon. Márinka came with her mother, carrying a parcel in her hand. She unwrapped it and held up a handsome red-and-white sash; Miss Elis took a similar one out of her wardrobe. Both of the students stood in the middle of the room, green caps braided with red and white on their heads. They had no uniforms, but shiny sabres, fastened to leather straps, hung from their hips.

Frybort bent his head smilingly and Márinka, blushing to the roots of her hair stood on her toes, fixing the sash across his shoulder and tying it safely above his waist. The student bowed and saluted. Suddenly the door opened and a very young student entered, saying he was to deliver a parcel to Mr Vavřena from Mr Brož. Vavřena reached out for it impatiently; another red-and-white sash was there, and when he unfolded it a letter fluttered to the ground. He picked it up and read it — and turned red with pleasure.

'Oh, I know I'll be turned down, I can see it coming,' Miss Elis said, 'but I don't mind standing aside. Mistress Lenka —'

'Sent me the sash.'

'Then I'll put mine away.'

'All right. But she would like you, Miss Elis, to fix this sash for me, if you don't mind.'

'On the contrary, I'll be proud to.'

The students thanked the ladies again and, saluting them, left to join the legion. The ladies went to the window and watched them as they walked away.

The revolution spread steadily, creeping even into Mr Roubínek's letters.

On that memorable Sunday Mr Roubínek sat behind his table, writing to his colleague in Rychmburk. At all other times the sentences seemed to form themselves with very little help from him, polished and tidy, a real pleasure for Mrs Roubínek to listen to. Today somehow Mr

Roubínek seemed unable to put two words together properly. Where was he to begin, what was he to write about, when so much was happening in these heathen, rebellious times. He was used to writing about the weather, news from the office, or some little item of gossip, but now? Mercy! Even his pen seemed intent on writing 'freedom, equality, the homeland, and abolition of serfdom.'

He had barely finished writing his first line when he was interrupted by noise and singing coming from the street outside, followed by marching steps. His wife and daughter rushed to the window.

'Daddy, oh daddy, here they come!'

The noise was, by now, right under his window, and Mr Roubínek left his chair and stood at the window too.

There were crowds of people in the street, the middle of which was taken up by the students' legion, marching in step, a captain at its head, another officer at the side of the ranks. All of them, without exception, wore green caps and carried arms.

Platoon after platoon passed, when Lottie suddenly moved in a startled way.

She had seen Vavřena who was an officer — and now she heard him giving a command:

'Eyes right!' The whole platoon presented arms.

'Eyes right!' followed command another given by Frybort for his friend's sake.

Whom could they have meant? Suddenly Lottie saw Vavřena look towards the window in the corridor, where she knew Lenka to be standing. The two platoons had saluted her!

She left the window quickly, at the same time as her father, who was making for his easy-chair in disgust.

Mr Roubínek picked up his quill again, as unsuccessfully as before. He put his right elbow on the table, waving

125

his quill in the air, and fixed his eyes on King Herod, a definite sign that he was deep in thought.

He could not get the legion out of his head. Patriots! Humph, patriots with green caps and arms. What a to-do!

He bent his head and started to write again. Green caps seemed to flow from the quill onto the paper. Who had ever heard of such a thing? There were no better Czechs than Žižka and the Emperor Joseph, and — arms and green caps indeed! Unheard of!

The students met for drill after their lectures. They were united at first, but the Germans among them who were known for their bossiness, had to leave the legion when the Czech majority would not stand for their bullying any longer. Thus the legion became completely patriotic under the leadership of an energetic youth, whose name was Jehlička.

Their patriotism went further than mere singing and shouting of slogans. Their lectures had all been in German until then, Czech as a language or as literature was almost unknown at college. Without exception they all felt the need to improve and perfect the command of their mother-tongue. Yet, was there anyone who could satisfy their need?

The teachers, one and all, were of an older generation and knew even less of the language and its literature, and not even Father Germanus could help them there, eloquent as he was.

Another meeting was held where it was decided unanimously to send a deputation, consisting of Vavřena and Frybort, to the dean's office, to see Father Antonius Šanta, who was known to be an honest and active patriot and who had, apart from that, studied and improved his knowledge of the language and its literature.

The young priest sat reading when the sabres rattled

in the corridor outside and the delegation entered the room. He was pleasantly surprised when he heard their request, and promised his help willingly on condition that the dean's permission was obtained. Under the circumstances there was no other way out for the dean — the new lecturer had to be approved.

A few days later the college's big hall was filled to overflowing; there were professors there, behind them students and guardsmen, and even the local townspeople had come to listen to the lecture. Only Father Germanus had ever attracted such a crowd up to that time — and only when his lecture had contained an especially important part of history. Could these be the same students who had caused such a riot only a year before? They stood in hushed silence, their eyes fixed on the young priest who ascended the dais.

He delivered the introduction in a ringing voice, reminding his audience of the glorious past of the nation, its victories and defeats, he spoke of the foremost fighters for the national revival, Jungmann, Šafařík and Palacký, and of the present hopeful times and of a better and brighter future.

The huge hall was as silent as a grave; the students listened with bated breath, their eyes aglow with fervour and enthusiasm. Father Antonius's eyes strayed to the white-haired Father Germanus, who rested his bent arms on his cane. His noble features showed plainly how deeply moved he was, while tears fell unheeded on his wrinkled cheeks.

This was indeed the joy of Simeon who had lived to see the dawn of a new day, for which he had waited for such a long time.

The hall shook with applause at the end of Father Antonius's lecture. From that day onwards his lectures

127

were included at the college, and no other lectures were so enthusiastically attended.

The same day on which the lecture took place which brought such pleasure to so many people, Mr Roubínek, who was not among the audience, was overtaken by a terrible misfortune.

Mrs Roubínek was unpleasantly surprised when she saw her husband's face on his return from the office. She pressed him to tell her the cause of his unhappiness — with no result. Mr Roubínek sank into his armchair, not bothering to take off Abraham first. Considering his thriftiness, this could indicate only real disaster. He sat there, turning his frosty glance upon King Herod and did not answer his wife's insistent questions until they turned into nagging.

'The Guards —'

'What about the Guards? Which Guards?'

'The Manor Guards —'

'What do you mean? I've no idea what you're talking about.'

'Manor Guards will be created.'

'*Aber Roubínek — rede doch vernünftig*, there are Guards in the town already.'

'I know, I know, but you see, Count George wants to have his own Guardsmen.'

At last Mrs Roubínek understood.

'*Du musst auch* — you mean, you'll have to join too?'

Mr Roubínek nodded.

'What about the notary? Will he have to join?'

'Yes, he and all the others too.'

What a topsy-turvy world! What could one expect from the lower classes if even the aristocracy took the rebels' part. But they were the masters, and one had to do

128

as one was told. He would have to go to the armoury where he would get an old sabre, a rifle, then he would have to stand in line and then, dear God! 'left, right, left, right' like a clown or the town's guardsmen or those crazy students. He, an official! And children and grown-ups would come and watch the drill and make fun of him if — God forbid — he should be out of step while jumping about like a clown, with a green cap on his head. What was to become of authority and respect?

11

The burning patriotism was drawing ever-widening circles, reaching farther afield with every new day. Even the ladies who had been indifferent until now, were carried by the stream. The seeds sown by the late Mrs Rettig were bearing fruit. As flowers seem to stretch and grow after a rainfall in the heat of summer, so patriotism blossomed forth under the shower of activities. The movement gave Miss Elis and Lenka the greatest joy. While the Guards and students were on drill parades and did their sentry duty, the matrons and spinsters collected money, with the proceeds of which they sewed and embroidered a beautiful flag, which was to fly above the heads of the students' legion.

The collectors were not very successful with the Roubíneks. Mrs Roubínek, who would have liked more than anything else to show them the door, gave them as small a contribution as she dared, knowing that in these troubled times she could not let them leave empty-handed. On the way down, the collectors met Mrs Roubínek's ward, who had obviously been waiting for them on the stairs. She took out of her pocket a small parcel and gave it to them with the words:

'Please accept this small gift from me.'

If Vavřena had seen his Lenka, so modest and so shy, he would have kissed her hands. She did not hesitate to sacrifice her small fortune for such a worthy cause.

May came again, this year without a festival. There was no time for it, more serious things were at stake. Fresh reports kept coming in from Prague, sometimes frightening people, but more often than not bringing hope of better times and a brighter future.

The action taken by the Litomyšl matrons and spinsters was a great success, the flag was ready and waiting. Lenka felt as happy as a child when Brož brought her a printed card which said, *'We have the honour to invite you to the solemn consecration of the flag of the Students' Legion in Litomyšl, which will be held on the twenty-first day of May, 1848, with the following programme.'*

Having read the programme, her eyes were arrested by the last few lines.

'The Sharpshooter Corps and the officers of the National Guards will enhance the celebration by their presence. Signed: The Committee of the Students' Legion in Litomyšl.'

She was happy and proud of Vavřena at the same time, for he was an officer and a member of the committee as well.

Meanwhile Mr Roubínek did something nobody would have ever expected him to do, considering his calm and icy manner.

On his return from drill parade, which had made him feel tired to death, he found the invitation on the table. He read only a few lines of it and, crushing the paper into a ball, threw it into the farthest corner. The fit of temper did him no good at all, for one cannot swim against the stream, and the celebration went on regardless of what he thought and felt.

The twenty-first of May was a cool day. In spite of

that, a large crowd of people collected at the college. Many people had assembled in the big hall: there were officials, the flag's sponsors, the young Count Kinský, students, and many other guests.

There, on an elevated dais, Father Germanus's niece, who was the flag's maid of honour, stood in festive dress, and presented the flag in the name of the girls and women of Litomyšl. Commander Jehlička replied in flowing terms on behalf of the students' legion. The whole crowd moved off to the town square afterwards, where the Sharpshooter Corps, the Guards and the students took up their positions.

Noisy and prolonged cheering rose to the clear sky when the newly consecrated flag, on which 'Unity and Equality' had been embroidered in gold, fluttered high over the heads of the students' legion, when the splendid streamers rippled in the wind for the first time.

Miss Elis and Lenka stood at the open window, watching the whole celebration with keen interest. They felt moved by the solemn silence, disturbed only by the priest's voice and later by the fervent cheers.

With the first sounds of music all the corporations and the crowds behind them formed a long procession and walked back to the Piarist Church, where the celebration was to be closed by Mass and the Te Deum. Miss Elis looked happily at the many rows of students marching proudly under the new flag; a slow flush spread across Lenka's features when a good-looking young officer glanced up and smiled a greeting to her.

Far from abating, political activity grew day by day. All feelings, be they apprehension, fear or pleasure, spread from Prague to the whole Kingdom. Unexpected changes occurred almost overnight, which together with news

132

from abroad weighed heavily on everybody's mind. Elections were to be held to the Czech Diet as well as to the Parliament of Frankfort, Palacký issued his famous manifesto. Czechs and Germans who had lived together peaceably enough suddenly found they could not get on any more. Prague witnessed quite a number of outrages and riots. The authorities lost control completely and wicked people misused the short era of golden freedom for their own ends.

Even Litomyšl, a quiet town in normal times, felt the wave of violent upheaval and unrest. Mr Roubínek was in despair; he was past grumbling and complaining, but took part in drill parades, went to his office or lounged about at home in his arm-chair, looking at his beloved picture — he did all that without a word. He unburdened his heart when his friend, the notary, visited him, for he could tell him all that was on his mind. Mrs Roubínek and her friend, the Roller woman, guarded their tongues carefully. Though they disapproved most heartily of everything they saw, it was dangerous to speak openly in such uncertain times.

Mrs Roller, who felt like a monarch deprived of his throne, voiced her protests only in whispers.

Lottie found it rather difficult to decide whose part to take. Since she hated to be in agreement over anything with Vavřena and Lenka, she would naturally have a view opposed to theirs; but all her contemporaries had changed and she found herself very much alone. Lenka, on the other hand, found her luck changed in her favour. She now had the opportunity of seeing Vavřena more frequently without any possibility of interference from her aunt.

They spoke of many things, of their love and hopes and better times to come, they discussed the present situation, and once Lenka said with a sigh:

'I wish uncle could have lived to see all this!'

'Yes. He would have crossed out what he wrote in the almanac.'

'If it weren't for the almanac —'

The students supplied Miss Elis with news all the time. Frybort gave her a real shock when he told her that this year's course of philosophy would terminate at the end of May, and this bit of news was an even greater shock to Márinka. Frybort, however, knew how to bring the light of happiness back into her eyes: he told her he would stay on. He intended to do so for her sake, but apart from that also because he wanted to see things through at Litomyšl.

Everything turned out differently than expected. He had to say good-bye quite unexpectedly, much sooner than he had intended to, and so did Vavřena, who had also meant to stay on in Litomyšl.

Some of the legionaries dispersed, especially after the eighth of June, when Jehlička in a public speech took leave of his colleagues and teachers and the patriotic citizens of the town.

'In the name of all my brethren, I take this oath: I swear to all those who died for our better future in the glorious past of our nation, to all those who died by the murderous hands of foreigners and intruders that we are true and faithful sons and that we shall defend the newly acquired rights of our nation with courage and with valour, that we will prove by our deeds that we are willing to honour our mother-tongue and our customs and traditions, and that we will defend them with our lives, should that prove necessary.'

Many a young lady shed tears when the brave philosophers dispersed. Márinka and Lenka were not among them, for they had nearly two whole months of happiness before them.

Then came the twelfth of June, the unlucky, fateful Whit Monday.

On the thirteenth of June dreadful news reached Litomyšl, creating a stir among the population. 'A revolution has broken out in Prague, terror reigns in our ancient city. Marauders rob and plunder, terrible confusion reigns everywhere, there are no means and forces to restore law and order.'

This and similar news, full of the most awful details spread like wildfire through the town. Crowds of people surged to the hill, guardsmen and sharpshooters mingling with ordinary citizens. It was reported that help was being sent to Prague from the surrounding countryside, and after a lengthy discussion it was decided to follow suit. First of all, however, several leading citizens were sent to the nearest railway station to find out how matters stood and whether Prague was getting help also from other towns. They left towards evening and were to return the following morning.

Two students left the open-air meeting before it was half-way through, having stayed just long enough to hear the vital points. They walked side by side, immersed in serious discussion and, upon arrival at Miss Elis's house, they shook hands cordially. Vavřena took the shortest path to the Manor, whereas Frybort went upstairs to Miss Elis's room, where he found his landlady in conversation with Márinka. Both of them showered questions on the student, feeling a little apprehensive by the serious expression on his face which, however, looked not at all downcast. Miss Elis turned pale when Frybort explained the situation, and Márinka burst into tears, and through her tears indistinct murmurs were audible:

'You don't love me, otherwise you couldn't leave me just like that —'

135

Frybort took her in his arms and spoke tender and consoling words, telling her it was his solemn duty to go, and anyway, he had promised Vavřena he would.

Miss Elis, too, tried to dissuade him, saying that his presence or absence could make no difference whatsoever to the outcome of the fight, and at any rate, what would his father say. However, neither her arguments nor Márinka's tears could shake his decision.

Lenka and Vavřena stood in the Manor park. She was listening with ever-growing fear to his whispered words, her eyes cast down to the ground. When he fell silent finally, she stood motionless for a while, every feature expressing sorrow and unhappiness, while a battle raged within her heart.

At last she looked up again with eyes brimming over with tears, and held out her hand to him.

'I know you can't act otherwise and apart from that... it — it's your duty to go.' Her voice broke and, putting her head on his shoulder, she sobbed heartbreakingly.

A sad night followed an unhappy evening. The light shone far into the night from Miss Elis's window; it was well past midnight when the front-door creaked as two men left. Upstairs Márinka shed bitter tears, while Miss Elis's lips moved in silent prayer. Lenka too was wide awake. She sat in her little room, an open book in front of her, containing 'A Prayer for my Country', written by her uncle's hand.

The members of the deputation sent out to make enquiries at the nearest railway station were galloping back to Litomyšl at dawn to pass on every bit of information they had gleaned.

They noticed neither Vavřena nor Frybort as they passed them on the road.

As the riders approached the town they met platoons

136

of guardsmen and sharpshooters who had decided to wait no longer and to march to Prague. Carts, laden with food, clothing and arms, in fact with all the wherewithal of this small citizens' army, stood outside Babka's Inn. The news which had been gathered at the station only confirmed what they already knew: that guardsmen from other towns were on their way to Prague. And so they, too, marched off.

At that time Mr Roubínek was girding himself with an old-fashioned sabre, in preparation for the defence of Prague. He felt sure that although he knew no better patriots than Žižka and the Emperor Joseph, they had not been forced to arm themselves like this. Mr Roubínek was pale with fear; he was terror-stricken, and it took him ages to fasten his belt. His spirits sank even lower at his wife's tears and his daughter's lamentations.

What a heartless fellow Count George was. On hearing that lawlessness had gained the upper hand in Prague, that lives and property were exposed to danger, that the Guards of Litomyšl and other towns had marched to Prague to help the cause, he had given orders to his own Guards to arm themselves with all dispatch and march off to Prague at once.

Oh King Herod! Your cruel butchery of white and black infants was mild indeed compared to this!

Mr Roubínek, to whom order and discipline were law, who lived in terror of unrest and disorder, was to take up arms against a mob and shoot! What if they should catch him, dear God, what would they do to him, those violent, mad rebels? For a certainty they would hang him on the nearest lamp-post and — unbearable thought — tear him limb from limb. What had he ever done to anyone that he, the most law-abiding of all citizens should be forced to have blood on his hands! Good-bye you quiet restful room with all your comforts, good-bye King Herod whom I might never see again, good-bye!

He embraced his wife and daughter, his face as pale as death, his cold eyes full of tears; he stumbled down the stairs, his sabre rattling against them with every step he took.

Count George's personal Guards were on parade in the courtyard. The members of the Guards, officials all of them, were fully armed and ready to march off. Their families and friends stood there waiting to see them off.

Suddenly the Count appeared and Mr Roubínek held his breath, expecting to hear words of command. The Count talked to his steward instead, and both of them looked towards the road to Mýto. What an unbearable moment of suspense. The Count had dispatched a special messenger to find out in detail how things stood, and no word had come from him so far; what if the Count should become impatient and, not waiting for his return, tell them to march off? Oh, if God in His great mercy would make the messenger bring glad tidings! Roubínek sighed and turned his eyes towards his family; there — there was the messenger all of a sudden, out of breath, sweat pouring down his brow. The Count was listening to what he said, interrupting him with questions now and then. All eyes were turned to the little group. Roubínek held his breath again — now — the Count was turning back towards the Guards and said that there was definite news that a revolution had broken out in Prague and that everything was in confusion there. 'There goes my last hope,' thought Mr Roubínek, 'now we'll really have to go.'

But, the Count continued in his speech, as the people had taken up arms against the Emperor and his army, he, the Count, or any of his people would have no part in it.

They were therefore free to go back to their homes and offices.

This piece of news was so unexpected that Mr Roubínek could hardly take it in. Events had taken so many unforeseen turns that he was unable to express his happiness and joy. He was the first to break ranks and, forgetting his dignity, he hurried over to where his wife and daughter stood.

Arrived at home, he unfastened the sabre and took his cap off while walking up the stairs. As soon as he was in his room he sank into his chair exhausted, but he had little or nothing to say.

12

During the night of the
fourteenth of June the armed forces left Prague secretly,
and occupied Hradčany, the castle. A state of siege was
declared by Prince Windischgrätz the next day. The people
took up the uneven fight, aiming their shots across the
river, to which the army replied with heavy artillery fire.

Vavřena and Frybort were in the fighting ranks, but
they had been separated; Vavřena was in a group of
students and took an active part in the shooting.

'Over here, friends!' a powerful voice called, and
when Vavřena turned round he saw a tall lean monk,
dressed in a coarse brown frock. The face of the youthful
monk was pale and not at all handsome, but his eyes shone
with a fanatical light. In his left a smoking rifle, he pointed
with his right hand to an endangered, empty spot.

'Špína!' Vavřena cried and hurried over to his friend.

'Ah, Vavřena, welcome! We'll talk later, now take up
your position over here.'

They rushed to the spot which the fearless monk
pointed out to them. He, in the meantime, was reloading
his rifle. Vavřena stood next to him; the noise of shots, the
whining of grenades, the groans of the wounded and the
dying filled the air with a turmoil of sounds. This certainly

140

was neither the time nor the place to start a conversation, and Špína only asked:

'Is Frybort here too?'

'Yes, he is.'

At that very moment a grenade fell nearby, sending splinters and earth in all directions. When the air cleared again after the explosion, many a young man who had held a rifle only a minute before, lay in a pool of blood.

Vavřena, having escaped unharmed, turned to look for Špína and saw him lying on the ground. He knelt down beside him and saw that he was dying. His face was white and a red stain was slowly spreading across his frock.

He carried the fatally injured monk to a sheltered spot with the help of another student.

Špína came to when medical aid had been given and spoke with great difficulty:

'Get back to the fighting, Vavřena, you're of much more use there than here. If you ever get back to Litomyšl, give my regards to — well — you know —' He fell back. Vavřena stayed with him until he breathed his last.

Thus the 'poor orphan' was not alone in his last hour, but had a friend by his side, a friend who mourned him honestly and sincerely.

This occurred on the fifteenth of June. An honourable capitulation was accepted on the following day, but Windischgrätz gave orders to resume the shooting when the army was fired on from one of the mills. The mills and waterworks were burnt to the ground.

Prague surrendered on the seventeenth of June. The army swooped down on the town and mass arrests began.

The troops from Litomyšl returned home before Prague surrendered and events took such an unfortunate turn.

141

Miss Elis made cautious enquiries, but nobody seemed to be able to give her definite news of her students. No one had seen them, although they had certainly been on the barricades and there had either been killed or arrested and sent for trial.

Lenka's face was drained of colour. Fear and loneliness had become her ever-present companions. There was nobody to whom she could turn to unburden her heart, for she had been forbidden to visit Miss Elis. She could not leave the house at all now that her uncle lay ill, because she had to wait on him as well as doing her normal household duties. Neither her aunt nor her cousin ever heard her sigh or utter a word of complaint.

She shed her ever-ready tears in the privacy of her own room, where she wept night after night as though her lonely heart would break.

Mr Roubínek fell dangerously ill.

'We can thank the new constitution for all our worries and troubles,' Mrs Roubínek said to Mrs Roller who had just returned from a prolonged stay with friends, and whose first visit was paid to Mrs Roubínek. She told her how badly Prague was damaged and how the rebels were being caught and brought to trial.

Mr Roubínek's face brightened noticeably when he heard this piece of news. 'Let's hope order will be restored again —'

The town was buzzing with rumours about Vavřena and Frybort, although Miss Elis and other friends of theirs spread the tale that they had gone home on vacations. Nevertheless it was said here and there that they had gone to Prague and stayed there, to which Mrs Roubínek added:

'Mr Roubínek was quite right when he said that Vavřena *ein schlechtes Ende nehmen wird.*'

A few days went by with no news whatsoever.

142

Six days had passed since the return of the town's detachment from Prague. Miss Elis went to bed in the evening as usual, but was suddenly awakened from a sound sleep later on at night.

She heard a familiar knocking on the door, the way Frybort used to knock when he came home late from an evening at Prent's Inn. She thought for certain that she had dreamt it, when the knocking was repeated, this time with greater urgency.

She got up trembling, dressed quickly, and hurried downstairs.

'Who is it?' she asked, her voice shaking.

'I, Miss Elis, Frybort.'

'Mother of God!'

She opened the heavy door to let him in. Frybort grasped her hand and shook it, then he himself shut the door again.

'Let's go upstairs quickly.'

Miss Elis lit the lamp and almost cried out in dismay. Was it possible that this was the healthy, happy youth she had known? Oh, how incredibly he had changed! How thin he looked in his torn and dirty clothes!

'Don't worry, my dear Miss Elis, I'm perfectly all right, I'm only awfully hungry. I've been on the road for four days. You see, I escaped from Prague and had to hide. Will you give me something to eat, please? How is Márinka?'

When Miss Elis brought him food, he asked her to wake up Márinka, because he would have to be on his way in a short time again.

Miss Elis was utterly confused. She felt happiness and fear surge through her simultaneously, and did whatever Frybort wished.

'Do you know anything at all about Mr Vavřena?'

'He's alive and well and on his way home. At first we

143

fled together, but then he went on to the mountains and gave me a letter for Lenka. You will give it to her, won't you. Špína, poor fellow, got killed on the barricades.'

Miss Elis was shocked and it took her a few minutes to grasp that Špína was dead. Had there been time, she would have expressed her sympathy and asked interminable questions. However, she had to go and wake up Márinka and her mother as quietly as possible, telling them only the barest details. They dressed hurriedly and hastened upstairs. When Frybort saw his Márinka at last, he forgot her mother's presence and embraced her with all the fervour of his youth. Márinka's mother was about to give him a talking-to for taking part in the uprising and perhaps even spoiling his chances of studying, but the student knew how to appease her.

He had almost forgotten that this was only part of what he had meant to do that night, when the churchbells struck two o'clock and brought him back to reality. He explained his position as far as time permitted, before saying good-bye to them. He left, making for the nearby Moravian border, after having promised to write as soon as he was safely home. He had come silently, in the middle of the night, and left again, unnoticed by anyone.

The following evening Lenka's room did not witness any more tears. She bent her head, and by the light of her candle re-read the note telling her that Vavřena was alive and well, that he had managed to escape, and that he would soon write to her again.

The uprising in Prague had been suppressed, trials and sentences followed in its wake.

Špína was well out of it. He had not suffered too long in his frock, the wearing of which had given him no joy at all, but he had to meet his Maker in it just the same.

144

Mrs Roubínek and her daughter received a great blow before the end of vacations. Mr Roubínek passed away. He left a will, which was of course in perfect order as was to be expected, and directed what was to be his wife's and what was to be his daughter's, what was to be done with the 'Colonel', 'Abraham' and the 'Tattler'. A special paragraph dealt with the 'valuable' picture of King Herod, on which his eyes had been fastened even on his deathbed. He bequeathed it to his dear friend, the notary, with whom he had had so many cosy talks. Not even Lenka was entirely forgotten in the will. A small sum was her inheritance in acknowledgement of her faithful services during his last illness.

Mr Roubínek had a magnificent funeral. The Lord had not seen fit to let him live long enough to have the pleasure of seeing order and discipline restored once more. Instead of that He had recalled him to enjoy the company of Žižka and the Emperor Joseph, 'and the church was a memorial of them'.

Miss Elis's flat was not as full of life as it was usually at this time of the year, even when vacations were over. Only three young students lodged with her. In spite of that, however, she felt content, for her wish had come true at last.

Her suggestion that Lenka move her things and come and live with her was accepted after Mrs Roubínek's initial objections were overcome. After all, they were related in a way.

Frybort, accompanied by his father, arrived after the vacations and asked for Márinka's hand. Her mother had dreamt of a doctor's title for her future son-in-law, but Frybort preferred the beautiful estate in the most fertile part of Moravia, which was his home, and Márinka had no objections.

145

'You loved a student and an officer, will you be able to love a farmer too?'

For an answer she embraced him.

Letters from Moravia were now addressed directly to Márinka; Miss Elis only got letters from Prague, and those were meant for Lenka. They were written by Vojtěch Vavřena, *medicinae studiosus*. He had escaped investigation as if by a miracle and could continue with his studies.

Zelenka did not write at all.

Carneval of the following year saw Frybort in Litomyšl again. He brought many guests who were all present while Márinka became his lawful wedded wife. Vavřena came from Prague to be best man, Lenka was maid of honour. When the bride hat cut the wedding cake, when toasts had been proposed to the happy pair and the mood was at its gayest, Vavřena rose from his chair and proposed a toast to the memory of their friend, who had met his death fighting for their common cause that fateful day on the barricades. The bride averted her eyes, Miss Eli shed a few tears.

13

The year 1849 passed. The college of philosophy in Litomyšl was closed down, the legion dispersed, its flag destroyed. The dean himself tore it from its pole and used the pole to support a gooseberry bush in the Piarist gardens. The Roller woman left the town and moved in with relations elsewhere.

Five years passed. The ancient house in which Miss Elis lived came to life again suddenly. Her dream came true, Lenka's desire was fulfilled. Vojtěch Vavřena, M. D., was getting married, leading the priest's niece to the altar at last. Their love was as fresh and sweet as it had been at the beginning of their courtship. They had guests from as far as Moravia, Frybort, happy and contented with his Márinka. Smiling happily, he said: 'I know you acted as best man at my wedding, pal, but I'm afraid I can't repay the service in kind, considering this,' and he pointed to his three-year-old budding son. Mrs Roubínek had been invited to the wedding, but did not put in an appearance.

Her pretty daughter had not found a husband yet for all her good looks and money. She waited for her Prince Charming, so far with no success at all.

Miss Elis moved in with 'her children', an action she never had any cause to regret. Now, even more often than

147

before, she would recount her old, old tale that fifty-one students had lived under her roof, of whom fifty had made their way in the world and the fifty-first had died a hero's death on the barricades.

While living with the Vavřenas she received a letter on which she had to pay a whole nickel. Who could that be writing to her out of the blue? The letter was from Zelenka, telling her that he was in a Monastery, where he was more than content. 'I don't have to live on bread and fruitstew any more,' he wrote among many other things.

'I can well believe that,' Vavřena commented. 'Most probably he has fat rosy cheeks and a rounded tummy, and doesn't even know what a book looks like any more, except his breviary.'

'I expect he also holds on to his money. He didn't even pay the postage!'

Christmas Eve came, the first Vavřena shared with his beloved wife. He received a charming letter from Frybort, in which a large sheet of paper, headed 'Fellow-students!' was enclosed. The letter itself said:

'This is the first copy of the manifesto we composed together before the memorable *Majales*. I found it at the bottom of my old trunk, and I thought you might like to have it in memory of old times.'

'I'm delighted to have it. Do you remember, Lenka? That was the year we met at the dear old tree, with its little bird's nest. We have our own nest now just like those birds had. And we're happy together, aren't we?'

Thus ends the legend of times gone by, set down to give pleasure to all my readers — the old ones, because they might remember some of it, and the younger ones because they might enjoy reading about it. At least I, the author, hope so.

A Poetic Idyll
and
Historical Reality

Alois Jirásek (1851—1930), author of historical novels, short stories and dramatic works, wrote the humorous, if somewhat wistful students' idyll *Gaudeamus Igitur* when he was 27 years old and when he had been teaching history at the secondary school in Litomyšl in Eastern Bohemia for four years. If he is sometimes called the Czech Walter Scott, then this is rather an expression of the fact that the Scottish romantic had been known in the country since the second decade of the nineteenth century, though more as a poet. Many decades passed before his novels were translated into Czech from the original, and before they took the place of the highly popular German historical novels. It was only then that Jirásek's generation, after Shakespeare, Milton, Byron, Goldsmith and Dickens, learned of Scott as a novelist. Accordingly, if Jirásek was compared to Walter Scott, it was a manifestation of the prominence he had achieved in Czech literature through his historical prose. If we were to accept this comparison, then we could best compare his *Gaudeamus Igitur* with Scott's novel *Waverly* — a history of the period sixty years before. Jirásek did not know the events of the revolutionary years 1848—1849 through personal experience, just as Scott only knew of the last Scottish rebellion through the narrations of eye-witnesses. In both cases, it was the first successful work in the elected *genre*. That, however, is as far as the similarity goes.

The Scott penchant was a coalescence of romantic entanglement and realistic description, chiefly of Scottish background. Jirásek proceeded similarly, but never denied in himself the history graduate of the University of Prague.

Sir Walter Scott attempted, at the decline of his life, to write popular historical works. Jirásek never completed the novel *Hussite King*, about George of Poděbrady, because reality and fiction had lost their connection. First and foremost, however, Scott was never the spokesman of Scottish nationalism, whereas Jirásek's literary works were of an instructive nature in that they consciously centered on the periods he considered the most important in national history — the period of Hussite Bohemia and that of the so-called national revival, the process of creating a modern Czech nation. Jirásek's extensive frescoes of the life of the little people in the Bohemia of the eighteenth and the first half of the nineteenth century are equally well produced as the scenes from Scottish life one finds in Scott's *Guy_Mannering* or *The Antiquary*.

However, how do Jirásek's 'Border' or 'Midlothian' appear? This is best answered by the rural area of Eastern Bohemia, where Jirásek was born into a family, half weavers, half farmers, where he spent the greater part of his youth and adult years until 1888, when his success as a writer opened up the gates of Prague, the capital not of an independent state but a province of the Austro-Hungarian Empire, ruled by the Habsburgs.

The region between the wooded hilly countryside at the Bohemian and Moravian border and the peaks of the Orlické and Krkonoše Mountains was not without significance in the history of the country. At Litomyšl, Jirásek's sphere of activity, an episcopate had been established five hundred years before, the first one to follow Prague. Even though it was later abolished, it was no accident that the most important centre of the Hussite revolution, after Prague and Tábor, was Hradec Králové, and that the Union of Bohemian Brethren was formed at the end of the fifteenth century in these hidden mountain valleys. It was the town of Litomyšl in which the Brethren carried on their diverse cultural activities, and in which so many of their first texts were published. This was at the time when many of the towns in Eastern Bohemia were acquiring fame as manufacturers of cloth which, in the sixteenth century, found a market in Austrian Linz and Vienna as well as Polish Cracow. Indeed, an important trade route led through Eastern Bohemia, which Richard Rowlands described in 1576 in his book, *The Post of the World*, a journey from Nuremberg through Plzeň, Prague and Náchod to Wroclaw and further still to Gdansk, or to the 'wild eastern regions'. Over this route travelled Bohemian cloth and hats, and back to the country there came 'Polish' cattle, fish from the Baltic, and Russian furs. But Eastern Bohemia, even though her agricultural production was not without significance, possessed at that time still another noteworthy form of income. This was linen production in Bohemia, Lusatia and Silesia from the last third of the sixteenth century. The products of Bohemian weavers found their way to Amsterdam, Haarlem and London through Nuremberg and later especially through Zittau, Leipzig and Hamburg. For the English and Dutch merchants very soon proved able to push their German competitors into the background.

150

The manufacture of cloth, linen and yarns gave sustenance to the inhabitants of the towns and villages, and contributed substantially to the prosperity of the authorities. In Litomyšl, Náchod, Opočno, Nové Město nad Metují, lofty Renaissance castles arose, solid town halls and churches, schools, hospitals and spa centres were built. The affluent notables of the day possessed sufficient means and time for politics. Their sons took pleasure trips through Europe. These feudal lords were not forced to seek each penny so pertinaciously and were only concerned with those branches of agriculture which produced a profit. They devoted themselves to building fishponds and breweries and usually had no interest in driving the peasantry into statutory labour and robbing them of their land.

All this was changed by the Thirty Years' War. It is true that the great military figures, among them the Trčkas of Náchod and their powerful ally, Albrecht of Waldstein, (Wallenstein), up to the downfall of the great Imperial commander in 1634, farmed in the old manner and were able to save their serfs from the worst extortion by the soldiery. But Waldstein was forced to administer brutal punishment to the Eastern Bohemian rebels who fought the Habsburgs with guns in hand under banners bearing the Hussite chalice. Then followed the pillaging of the Waldstein and Trčka estates, and in place of the old feudal lords there came new masters whose appetites were far greater and who did not want to wait long. These were either military adventurers or members of Austrian or Italian feudal families who had helped the Habsburgs to defeat the rebellious Bohemian Estates in the years 1618—1620, and who were rewarded with manorial estates. In Eastern Bohemia, the Trautmannsdorfs received Litomyšl, the Coloredos Opočno, the Piccolominis Náchod. Among those who received their reward here were the Scottish and Irish perpetrators of the murder of Waldstein at Cheb, the Leslies and the Butlers.

In the middle of the seventeenth century, the Belgian Jesuit des Haies condemned with horror the conditions which were prevalent in the Krkonoše Mountains after the war. The new lords acquired a great deal of the land but meagre manpower. Their treasuries were empty and their needs were great. And so the feudal lords chained their subjects to the land, making their position similar to that of the serfs in the period of the early Middle Ages.

The reaction to this upheaval in economic and social development set in soon. The great Peasant Uprising of 1680 had its core here, in the environs of Litomyšl and Náchod, and it spread from this part of the country to engulf almost the whole of Bohemia. The great peasant rebellion was suppressed by troops commanded by the sons of the old as well as the new feudal families.

Today we know, of course, that though this process of new feudali-

151

zation plunged the development of Bohemia a century back and brought immoderate poverty and grief to whole generations of the people of Bohemia, it could not turn the wheel of development back. Two decades after the Uprising of 1680, some of the feudal lords found that profits from linen and cloth were far greater than those from working the frequently unfertile small fields in the mountains and the valleys. This did not mean that they wanted to mitigate their demands, on the contrary. And so the life in the mountains and the valleys continued on in great hardship. In the mountains smuggling gained ground and in the valleys the weavers, cloth-makers, glass-makers and the forge workers suffered poverty and want.

Poverty had its permanent home here even though other disasters did not come, among them wars in the first place. In the middle of the eighteenth century, part of the battles between Austrian and Prussian regiments took place in the neighbourhood of the newly-built Fortress of Josefov, bearing the name of Emperor Joseph II. In an effort to amass troops for the fight against his Prussian opponents, Joseph II and his mother and predecessor, Maria Theresia, introduced extensive reforms of the state administration which made of their manifold domain a uniform state body in accordance with the conceptions of 'enlightened despotism'. Whether they liked it or not, this affected the structure of society; with a greater view to the economic needs of the middle class and the abolition of serfdom in the villages (1781).

Joseph's reforms, also forced through by the famine at the beginning of the 'seventies and the great Peasant Uprising of 1775, whose starting point lay again in the East Bohemian Krkonoše, ended in a transformation of the state organization in Habsburg lands and opened the doors wide to far-reaching social changes. The monarchy of the Austrian Habsburgs continued to be the last form of a feudal state, a feudal absolutist monarchy, in which the decisive position of the monarch was conditioned by a definite balance of power between the feudal lords and the fast rising bourgeoisie.

The members of the old ruling class were none too pleased with this, and the 'Bohemian Estates' opposition to the 'revolutionary Emperor' was led in Bohemia by two noblemen of Irish descent, William MacNeven and Count Taaffe. An oddity of Austria as a multi-national state was the fact that from the end of the eighteenth century there was not just one bourgeoisie — the Austrian — in the process of formation under the monarchy, but also a Czech, Italian (Lombardy, Venice) and others. The development of the Czech bourgeoisie was undoubtedly more difficult than that of its Austrian rival. Joseph's reforms facilitated the process of creating a modern Czech nation. Basing themselves on the aspirations of the Czech national element were also representatives of the 'Estate' opposition, who were not aimed against the dead Joseph II, but against the reactionary current which held sway at the Viennese Court, mainly during the reign of Joseph's nephew, Franz I. It is characteristic, however, that under the reign of Franz I and his omnipotent first Minister, Prince Metternich, the combined power of the feudal lords and the Catholic Church, was unable to abolish even one of the more important of Joseph's reforms.

Neither Franz nor Metternich could do without the representatives of financial circles, particularly in the period of the great struggle with Napoleonic France and later when the great powers ruled Europe through diplomatic congresses. The original five, made up of Austria, Russia, Prussia, Great Brittain and France, were soon broken up by their diverse attitudes towards the emancipation movement in various European coutries. British diplomacy at the congress in Opava (1820) dissociated itself from the plan of intervention against revolutionary Naples, France still took on the task of intervening in Spain, but the fight of the Spanish colonies for independence and the Greek uprising against the Turks definitely separated both 'maritime' powers from the 'Triple Alliance', strengthened in 1833 at a meeting in Mnichovo Hradiště in Bohemia. Austria, Russia and Prussia continued to guard the continental core of Europe against all dangerous revolutionary movements, chiefly in Poland, Italy and the Balkans. The conservative principles of this Alliance were, however, alien to both the English and French people.

This meant that the Austrian government could not rely upon benevolent credit in England, which Austria had been receiving since the allied fight against revolutionary France. It is characteristic that those who had negotiated English credit for Austria became the victims of the cooling relations. The first was the banking house of the Parish Brothers in the middle of the 'twenties, originally of Leith, Scotland, who later had their headquarters first in Hamburg and, finally, in Vienna. The clash with the powerful Rothschilds was fatal for the Parishes. With what was left of the family fortune, they bought a country estate in Eastern Bohemia and retired completely from banking and industrial undertakings, which were subsequently dominated by their more fortunate rivals, who continued to finance the Metternich regime up to 1848.

Not only the Parishes and the Taaffes, but other feudal lords as well perceived their model in the English aristocracy even during the chill in Anglo-Austrian relations, and did all they could to imitate their way of life.

More important still, some of the Austrian aristocracy realized that the process of industrial revolution, which had made England the first great world power, would in time overflow into Europe. For these people, too, England was the model, but for other reasons than her

153

aristocracy. Archduke Rudolph, brother of Emperor Franz, Archbishop of Olomouc in Moravia, laid down on his estates in Ostrava what proved to be the foundation of the later Vítkovice iron works. His adviser was Professor Riepl of the Vienna Technical School, who was a constant visitor to England and knew the inventor Stephenson personally. Through his efforts English and Welsh experts came to Vítkovice to work the new type of blast furnaces. Another group of smelters and foundry workers from South Wales came to North Moravia, where the Moravian governor of that time, Count Mittrowský, built the huge foundries in Sobotín and Štěpánov with their help. Count Mittrowský took great care to keep his valuable experts from leaving, and even had English books brought for them from England.

However, the feudal lords were not the only ones who went to England; many Czech chemists, technicians and engineers also went there. We find these people building the first Austrian railroad, leading from Vienna across Moravia to the Russo-Prussian border beyond Ostrava, with an important branch line from Olomouc to Prague. The part played by others was important particularly in the building of the first sugar refineries. Many an English expert settled down in Bohemia. In the 'thirties, a machine shop belonging to the Englishman Ruston opened in the Prague suburb of Karlín, not far from the slightly older machine shop of Evans and Joseph Lee. The Englishman Bracegirdle opened a machine shop in Brno in 1844 and the first machine shops in North Bohemian Liberec were similarly established. This, of course, was just the beginning of the rapid upsurge of industry in the Czech lands which followed after the 1848 revolution. The lives of the absolute majority of the Czech people in the villages and towns were almost untouched by the process of industrialization. With the exception of Prague and Brno, the first industrial plants were located in the border regions where there were sufficient supplies of water and fuel and where the majority of inhabitants were German. Even though the textile owners of Northern Bohemia had already weighed the possibility of expanding into Hungary and the Balkans, this was mostly wishful thinking. On the threshold of the revolutionary year 1848, those aligning themselves to the Czech national element besides the rural inhabitants were the petty bourgeoisie, engaged in the crafts and trade, and the intelligentsia, whose ranks were expanding speedily.

The Eastern Bohemian town of Litomyšl presented a good picture of Czech society on a small scale before 1848. It is characteristic that Jirásek had so little to say of the aristocratic occupants of the Renaissance castle belonging to the Waldsteins at the time. More important than life in the castle was the life in the town belonging to it. There, among other things, was the brewery in which the brewer was the father of the composer Bedřich Smetana. The scene of

Gaudeamus Igitur is the Piarist college, lying on the hill directly opposite the entrance to the castle. The work of the clerical teachers was, according to the custom of the day, to prepare the students of the 'Latin' secondary schools for study at one of the university faculties. The young 'philosophers' roughly supplemented their knowledge by the two-year study. There were a number of enlightened teachers at the Litomyšl college, and fervent Czech patriots who aroused national Czech feelings in their pupils were not lacking among them. But the 'upper class', the bourgeois notables, were still unenlightened. Most of them were bi-lingual and, of course, leaned rather towards German culture than education in the Czech language, drawing for reinforcement on the older national history or amassing its forces for the future advance.

We find, accordingly, a typical situation in Litomyšl. The world of feudal aristocrats was cut off from life in the town by the high walls of the castle park, a world which was cosmopolitan to the core and devoted to Austria and the Habsburgs despite the opposition mood. There is then in the town the bourgeoisie with its German veneer, the small groups of 'middle class Czechs,' and the Czech students coming from former serf families.

Did the English people know of this situation in Austria and did Bohemia know anything of England and her problems before 1848? The fate of the Czech people probably occupied the English liberals who, however, showed the same interest in the Czechs as they did in the Hungarians, the Serbs or the Albanians. This can be clearly seen in the wide interest of John Bowring, a one-time collaborator of Byron's (Patrick Taaffe of Bohemia, who lived with him at one time in Pisa), who wrote about Czech literature and established ties in the 'twentie with a circle of Czech writers around the poet F. L. Čelakovský. In 1832, Bowring published to selection of Czech poetry, *Cheskian Anthology*, dedicated to Čelakovský, and emphasizing not only the national, but also the political character of older and new Czech literature alike. In the 'thirties, the aquarelles of Samuel Prout, portraying the Czech countryside and the picturesqueness of Bohemia, particularly Prague, achieved fame. Richard Pocock (*Description of the East and Some Other Countries* II, 1833) felt that Prague was the most beautifully situated town in the world. B. A. Granville (1836) admired the beauty of the Bohemian spas and the wealth of the Bohemian feudal aristocracy. It was very important, though, that John Strong called attention to the new Czech literature, Czech music and the progress of the Czech industry as far back as 1831. G. R. Gleig, six years later, weighed the attitude of the Czech towards the Habsburgs (*Germany in 1836* by John Strong; *Bohemia and Hungary, Visited in 1837*). And quite a few Englishmen probably read the sharp attacks by Karel Postl, a native of South Moravia who, after running away from the

Prague Monastery of the Crusaders, wrote in America under the name of Charles Sealsfield. His books were widely read and were published in the English and German languages.

It is not too surprising that Czech readers learned far more of English literature and industrial and social conditions. Czech writers sought in England not only what was of interest, but what was of benefit to the development of Bohemia. Most of it, though, was information passed on, for except J. V. Frič, one of the Czech leaders who played a part in revolutionary activities, no one had been to England. It would, however, be correct to say that the little the Czech public knew of political terminology before the spring of 1848 was of English origin, and that England meant to the Czech public what France meant to Czech fashion and Germany to the young Czech philosophy.

In the winter of 1847, the economic crisis and widespread poverty caused political tension in a number of European countries. In England, the Chartists tried for the third time to push through their democratic programme, demonstrations against the regime of the 'bourgeois king' Louis Philippe multiplied in France, Italy was teeming, and neither the suppressed revolutionary movement in Polish Cracow nor the end of the civil war in Switzerland brought peace. The young Czech lawyer and future politician, F. L. Rieger, went to Italy at almost the same time as Metternich's confidant, Ficquelmont. Rieger had the opportunity there of 'studying the revolution', Ficquelmont was to bolster up the feeble Austrian position. The new year brought the revolution in Sicily and Naples, from where the Austrian envoy, Felix Schwarzenberg, was unceremoniously expelled. Even before Schwarzenberg arrived in Vienna, popular uprisings — patterned on the events which had taken place in February in Paris, Southern Germany and London — sprang up there and in Prague. The March revolution of 1848 swept away the old regime of Austria, banished Chancellor Metternich from Vienna and the country, and set up a government which was temporarily headed by Kolowrat-Libštejnský, Metternich's old adversary, with Pillersdorf and Ficquelmont as ministers, all belonging to the group of Metternich collaborators of long standing, all convinced of the need to make concessions to the revolutionary movement. And so March to June 1848 was a period when the Viennese government, urged on by the popular movement in Vienna in March and again in May of the same year, conceded step by step to the demands of the bourgeoisie, exploiting the dissatisfaction of the working people to exert pressure on the government. The workers and students in Vienna, in Prague and, to a lesser degree, elsewhere too — Litomyšl for example — constituted the vanguard of the victorious bourgeois revolution. A mood of intoxication prevailed in the spring of 1848 which sprang from the conviction that the fruits of the revolution could not be endangered. Hungary was in open revolt, the Austrian troops, under Radetzky's command, were driven out of Venice and Milan in Northern Italy and kept their foothold only under the protection of the great Lombardy fortresses. Also finding refuge there were the big feudalists, Felix Schwarzenberg among them, who were completely terrified by the 'anarchy' on their estates, where the serfs refused to perform statutory labour. It was not until the summer of 1848, when Radetzky succeeded in defeating the troops of the Sardinian King Carlo Alberto, that these people began to hope for the final defeat of the revolution.

It was only the more far-sighted of the Czech politicians who noticed the measures taken in Bohemia by members of the feudal-military group, headed by the new military commander of Bohemia, Prince Windischgrätz. They could not know that the old Chancellor Metternich, both in Brussels and in England, where he had paid a 'visit to good Doctor Brighton', had kept a watchful eye on developments in Austria and had made his influence felt on members of the government and the military authorities through some of the diplomats. Field Marshal Windischgrätz was hated in Prague because he had been bent on earning the reputation of 'strong man' in suppressing the first workers' revolts on Czech soil as far back as the summer of 1844. In Prague, a group of generals-estate owners which included, in addition to Windischgrätz, the Sunstenaus, the Lobkowiczes, the Schwarzenbergs and others, had been forming since 1844. The Prague 'radicals' saw quite correctly that a clash with these representatives of open reaction was unavoidable.

The liberal circles, led by Palacký were, therefore, unpleasantly surprised at the revolt which burst out at Whitsuntide in 1848 in Prague, in defence of the revolution which was threatened by the bayonets of Windischgrätz's grenadiers. The revolt was, of course, a welcome occasion for Windischgrätz and the other advocates of the 'strong arm' policy to smash the resistance of students and workers fighting on the barricades to defend the legacy of the bourgeois revolution of March. The old argument as to whether the Whitsuntide revolt was a happy step is, in the light of documents available today, quite futile. According to the testimony of General Joseph Lobkowicz, Windischgrätz counted firmly on 'saving the monarchy' with his troops and on squashing Prague, Vienna and Budapest in turn. The revolt was, therefore, the right step, the negative aspect being the political short-sightedness of the spokesmen of the Czech liberal bourgeoisie and the out-and-out treason of the conservative elements. Windischgrätz triumphed over the whole of the Czech national movement, but it is characteristic of the short-sightedness of the Austrian German-speaking bourgeoisie that they rejoiced in a spirit of pan-

157

Germanism at the defeat of pan-Slavism, while Windischgrätz was following a different purpose altogether — to defeat the revolution.

This was perfectly understood by Marx and Engels, but not by the spokesmen of the 'left-wing', i. e. the Austrian German-National Liberals in the Vienna Parliament, nor their adherents in the Bohemian and Moravian border towns with their German majority. The blindness of the pro-German burgeoisie in Northern Bohemia went so far in the summer of 1848 as to welcome Windischgrätz's successes almost as their deliverance from the Slavic 'deluge'. While representatives of the counter-revolution were negotiating in St Petersburg with Czar Nicholas I for help against the revolutionary elements, the German liberals were trying at the Congress of representatives of the bourgeois societies of Bohemia, held at Teplice Lázně in August 1848, to push through the division of the Bohemian territory into the 'Sudeten' and an interior region, wherein the first region would be an exclusively German territory which was to decide whether or not it would become part of the German Customs Union. The danger of these efforts, which did not take into account the changes brought about by the industrial revolution in these regions, was seen by the English observer Noel 'living near Děčín', who sharply criticized these attempts in the *Prague Official Gazette.*

The voices raised for co-operation of Czechs and Germans were negligible at the Teplice Congress. The voices of the Radical Democrats on both sides were ignored, and thus the way was cleared — for the military-feudal clique to take over power. The Prague and Milan centres of the counter-revolution came to an agreement sometime in August. Radetzky's victories bolstered up the self-assurance of the military powers, who had already drawn up a plan in August on how to occupy key positions at the Court and have the 'army take over the protection of the Court and the government' at the first possible moment. The detailed plan was realized in Vienna by the military adjutant of the Emperor Ferdinand, Lobkowicz, whose task it was to transfer the Court to the Olomouc fortress, commanded by Sunstenau, who was another member of the conspiracy. The part of liaison-officer between the generals in Lombardy and those in the Czech Lands was given to Windischgrätz's brother-in-law, Felix Schwarzenberg. He took part in October 1848, in suppressing the revolutionary movement in Vienna — the same Vienna which had rejoiced at the suppression of the Prague revolt — by the side of Windischgrätz. And it was the generals who installed Felix Schwarzenberg as Prime Minister in November, and who — with the approval of part of the Court camarilla — carried out the change in Olomouc at the onset of December, enthroning the youthful Franz Joseph I, in whom the Catholic hierarchy also had great hopes.

Of the revolutionary gains, there remained at the end of 1848 only the abolition of serfdom and the ancient patrimonial system. However, the large estate owners received compensation for the diminished labour. This was seen to by the German 'liberal', Dr Alexander Bach who, through the power of the estate owners, became a member of the Schwarzenberg government and, in the end, his virtual successor. Among the tasks of his future ministry, the Ministry of the Interior, were the gradual dissolution of the *Reichstag* in the winter of 1848, transferred from the insurgent Vienna to the provincial seat of the Archbishop of Olomouc, Somerau-Beekh, to Kroměříž. The Czech journalist, Karel Havlíček Borovský, commended the *Reichstag* for broadening the knowledge of English political terminology as late as December 1848 and, in truth, the records are full of such terms as 'budget', 'amendment', 'bill'. But the days of the *Reichstag* were numbered — at the beginning of March 1849 it was dissolved as a product of the revolution and as such unacceptable to the new rulers of Austria. The last attempt of the Czech and German radical democrats in the spring of 1849 to prevent the absolute triumph of the counter-revolution, was doomed to failure. The elderly Prince Metternich was able to return from England — moving to London and other parts of the world in his place were his young adversaries: the German radicals Meissner, Ebert and Hartmann, the Czechs Rieger, Straka and Springer. Rieger and Springer studied 'social conditions' in England — the revolution in Austria was smashed, but feudalism was broken in spite of that. The era of industrial revolution and rise of the bourgeoisie began in Central Europe.

It only remains for us, to look at the reaction to the revolution and counter-revolution in Bohemia and Austria as we see it reflected in the English press. If the liberal *Economist*, the semi-official *The Times* and the conservative *Morning Chronicle* uphold a line favourable to the German bourgeoisie and of little favour to the Czechs, in the spirit of an affinity of material interests, then the newspapers *Fraternal Democrats*, *The Northern Star* and the Chartist *Reasoner* and *Cause of the People* view the Czech question differently.

The *Economist* was completely dependent on its Leipzig correspondent, who disliked the Czechs intensely. The fight waged by the Czech workers and students on the barricades of Prague nevertheless forced him to own that the Slavs and Czechs, who were until then practically unknown, had begun some kind of national existence.

Still more markedly on the side of the German bourgeoisie was *The Times*. The fight against Windischgrätz's cold-bloodedly prepared reaction was, for this reason, described on the pages of *The Times* as 'the pillaging by the mob', as 'a war of two races', a bloody revolution worse than the Viennese, while the 'firmness and moderation' of the bloodthirsty Windischgrätz was praised.

The first small steps, and what moderate steps they were, of Czech national policy, accordingly did not find favour in the eyes of the English bourgeoisie, biased by material interests to maintain relations with German capital, and looking upon the Czechs and Slovaks with contempt. Surely it is not surprising that the attitude of the English Chartists on the 'Czech question' was exactly the opposite.

Their leader, Ernest Jones, published a poem in March 1848, called 'The March of Freedom'. In April, in the last issue of the *Labourer*, Jones commenced his series 'The Uprising of the Working Classes', a history of the Czech Hussites, perhaps under the influence of the Frenchman, Louis Blanc. The article was never completed. Other Chartists, (W. J. Lington, G. J. Holyoake) were influenced in their positive attitude towards the Austrian Slavs by the Italian revolutionary nationalist, Giuseppe Mazzini. Mazzini himself, in his article 'On the Slavonic Movement', drew heavily on the earlier expositions of Bowring. He influenced the Chartist poet, Thomas Cooper, who lectured on the theme, 'The Slavonic People - An Oration', in 1848, speaking on Hussite Bohemia, and on the Slovenes who inhabit Northern Hungary and their fight with the Hungarians.

The Litomyšl student of philosophy, Špína, dying on the Prague barricades, was unaware that the bloody battles of June 14th—17th, 1848, were the subject of discussion in far-away England. He was also unaware of the fact that he was taking part in a 'racial fight of the Czechs against the Germans' and the poor fellow would have fought the accusation that he was concerned only with terror and massacre. The British papers and their readers were taken in by German propaganda. This was possible, on the one hand, because the German trade partners were closer to the English bourgeoisie than the Czech people and, on the other, because despite the existence of sympathy between the Czech democrats and the English Chartists, there were no close connections, nor was there any exchange of information.

The gap in the knowledge of English readers can, at least, be filled in in a manner truly appropriate and, at the same time, charming by this work of Alois Jirásek. The history of the Czech year 1848 should stimulate all people of good will in the countries of Wycliffe and Huss to know more of each other, to follow their struggles just as the small handful of Czech democrats did in 1848, on the one hand, and the equally small handful of Chartists did on the other.

JOSEF POLIŠENSKÝ

NOTES

Ach, schau, Lottie	Oh, look Lottie
aber es ist so schön draussen	it's so lovely outside
Sie war hin vor Bewunderung	She was beside herself with admiration
Majales	Students' May Day festival
Diese Majales	This May Day festival
Es ist ihr Vorrecht	It is their privilege
.. so stolz, so könnte man ihn ausstehen	.. so proud, he would be quite bearable
Eifersucht	jealousy
Und weh dem Lande, dessen Söhne frech verachten Heimatstöne und heimatlichen Sagenkreis	Woe to the land whose sons hold in contempt their mother-tongue and despise their forebears' traditions
Aber alles!	Everything, though
Er kann es nicht ausstehen	He can't stand it
.. das gemeine Volk	.. the common people
.. komm, komm, mein liebes Kind!	.. come over here, my child!
Bedenke nur! die Leny!	Just imagine! Lenka!
Na, es wird sich zeigen	Well, we'll see
.. aber unbeholfen	but he's awkward and clumsy
.. keine andere	no one else
Wenn eine Dame schön sein soll muss sie schön gewachsen sein	A lady must have a nice figure to be beautiful
.. muss sie dunkle Augen haben	.. must have dark eyes
.. muss sie dunkles Haar haben	.. must have dark hair
Wie ich sag	As I said
Bedenke nur, wie er ungalant ist	Just think how discourteous he is
Diese Konstitution! You mark my words, man wird noch rauben und morden!	This Constitution! You mark my words, they'll plunder and murder yet!
Und was die Professoren und was der Pater Rector	And what about the teachers and the Father Rector
.. rede doch vernünftig	.. why don't you talk sense
.. ein schlechtes Ende nehmen wird	.. will come to a bad end

TRANSLATOR'S NOTES

PAGE 55 *Vivant professores*
Latin for 'long live the lecturers'.

PAGE 56 *Coniuratio*
Latin for 'conspiracy'.

PAGE 56 *Secessio*
Latin for 'rebelion'.

PAGE 59 *In silvis resonant...*
old Latin students' song. (The woods resound with sweet songs, the woods resound with a sweet song).

PAGE 70 Mrs Rettig
Magdalena Dobromila Rettigová (1785—1845) was one of the foremost Czech revivalists living in Litomyšl.

PAGE 76 *Vivat commissarius*
Latin for 'long live the commissar'.

PAGE 76 *Vivat doctissima*
Latin for 'long live the most learned'.

PAGE 76 *Vivat Xantippe*
Latin for 'long live Xantippe'. Xantippe was the wife of Socrates and is generally believed to have been a shrew.

PAGE 76 *Vivat Horatius Flaccus*
Latin for 'long live Horatius Flaccus' (ancient Roman poet).

PAGE 78 *Gaudeamus*
Latin for 'let us enjoy ourselves'.

PAGE 86 *Corpus delicti*
Latin term for the essential acts and facts relating to a certain crime.

PAGE 86 The poem *May*
written by Karel Hynek Mácha. The poem is very famous, and was sharply attacked by critics in those days.

PAGE 90 *Ex moribus primam, cetera eminenter*
Latin for 'behaviour satisfactory, otherwise top marks'.

PAGE 94 Count George
Jiří Kinský - aristocrat and landowner in Litomyšl.

PAGE 94 *Deus ex machina*
Latin for an unexpected outcome of a difficult and complicated situation.

163

DATE DUE

HIGHSMITH 45-102   PRINTED IN U.S.A.